If You Want to Live

a novel

by

Carolyn Orser Key

authorHOUSE™

1663 LIBERTY DRIVE, SUITE 200
BLOOMINGTON, INDIANA 47403
(800) 839-8640
WWW.AUTHORHOUSE.COM

First published by AuthorHouse 01/28/05

ISBN: 1-4208-2018-4 (sc)

Library of Congress Control Number: 2004195175

Printed in the United States of America
Bloomington, Indiana

This book is printed on acid-free paper.

For Michael

Acknowledgements

I owe a debt of gratitude to many people without whose help this book would have never seen the light of day:

To Dwight, for kicking me in the right direction and keeping me there;

To Sarah, for spending endless hours editing and listening to me whine;

To Kim, for sharing her insight and editorial expertise;

To Phyllis for honing my skills as a writer;

To my mother, Eloise, for giving me more than she will ever know;

To Mary, for keeping me honest;

To Bob and Suzi, Ed and Jo, for believing in their little sister;

To Glenn and Ellen, for donating the computer on which this book was written;

To Kendra, for sharing her wisdom on our morning walks in the woods;

To my children, Jessica and John, Kim, Terry, and Rebecca, and my grandson, Erik, for bringing joy and meaning to my life;

To my husband, Michael, for holding me tight and refusing to let go…

Chapter I

He told her to be there at 3:00. But, she purposefully left the apartment so as to arrive a little late. Walking from the bright afternoon into the dimly lit diner, she paused to let her eyes adjust, then glanced nervously around at the booths on either side of the door. All she saw were two gray-haired men talking loudly above their white ceramic cups of coffee, displacing the rising steam with their hand gestures -that, and the long empty line of stools in front of the counter, their torn red vinyl tops looking somehow abandoned.

A thin woman wearing a food-stained apron slouched against the cash register. She was smoking, or rather holding a lit cigarette with ash an inch long, staring through the dingy front window.

She had not seemed to notice Claire, but nodded with her head toward an empty booth beside the jukebox. Willing herself smaller, or, better, invisible, Claire walked toward the jukebox in that careful heel-to-toe step she had mastered as a child sneaking past her parent's bedroom when they were arguing. She slid into the seat facing the wall.

1

"Why is he making me do this?" Claire wondered. In her mind she could see him. She could see his familiar comforting face, his soft eyes that always looked directly at her, could hear the soothing tone of his voice that he used during her therapy sessions -as if he were talking to an abused animal, a stray he had rescued from the side of the road and hoped would not bite.

"You need to get out, Claire," he had told her during their last time together. "You need to see people." But seeing people, to her, meant being hurt. Still, how could she say no to this person, the only man, besides David, she had ever trusted?

So she had willed herself to this place filled with human smells, grease and fried meat —and something else that was not so pleasant -sweat maybe?

"He's not coming," Claire panicked. "Maybe this is some sort of test to lure me out and see how I act in public —alone and exposed." The thought made her heart beat faster and she reached back to retie her ponytail in case any stray hairs had managed to escape.

"Your hair looks fine, Claire," Mark had told her during one of their sessions. Until then she had been unconscious of this habit. He had spent the rest of the hour that day analyzing her need to stay in control, to bind up her feelings like those wisps of hair.

"What are you afraid of, Claire?"

She had burst into tears. "Of myself," she had blurted out.

"Of your anger, Claire?"

"Yes," she had shouted. "Are you satisfied?"

"We need to talk about this some more," he said, but the time was up. That was when he had suggested they hold their next session at the diner.

Claire glanced at her watch. 3:08. Was that all? "God, it seems like I've been here for hours," she thought. "If he doesn't come by 3:15, I'm leaving!"

"What can I get you, Hon?" the waitress' raspy voice startled her.

"Oh, oh...just coffee, thanks," she muttered, not knowing if she had actually spoken her last thoughts.

"Cream and sugar?"

Claire stared at the gray Formica tabletop, repeating the simple words to herself until she could discern their meaning, a strategy which had served her well in her high school French class.

"No, just black. I'm not staying long."

"Suit yourself." The waitress' words felt accusatory. Claire sank down lower in her seat so that the top of her head barely showed above the back cushion.

Why was it always like this? Like she had to apologize constantly for everything –even for being alive. Maybe she should have ordered a piece of pie, or something else that gave her the right to sit in this dirty booth and be waited on.

The waitress returned and set the mug in front of Claire along with a spoon and napkin. "Are you O.K., Sweetie?" she asked. This unexpected kindness brought tears to Claire's eyes. She tried to brush them away discreetly, pretending to adjust her makeup.

"Yes, I'm, I'm waiting for someone. He's late."

"Aren't they always." The waitress rolled her eyes, the lids caked with blue shadow. Claire noticed the deep lines fanning out from the corners, and tiny cracks beneath the blush on her sunken cheeks.

"It's nothing like that, really," Claire felt compelled to explain. "He's just my...friend." "Therapist" suddenly sounded so petty in the presence of this tough woman whose rough ring-less hands conveyed her share of life's bitterness.

"Some friend to keep you waiting...You just holler if you need a refill."

Claire turned to watch her walk away. Where does it come from, she wondered, that ability to knock life right back in the face?

She blew across the top of her coffee before taking a sip and welcomed the warm liquid as it slid down into her stomach. The muscles in her shoulders had just begun to relax when she felt a gentle pressure.

"Sorry I'm late." Claire recognized his voice before looking up. "Wouldn't you know it, the hospital called right as I was walking out the door with a question about a medication for one of my patients."

Claire could smell the cool outside air as he passed, sliding into the seat opposite. Her heart quickened, the way it always did in his presence, but she tried to make her voice sound nonchalant. "Oh, are you? I hadn't noticed."

"Good," Mark replied. "See, getting out has already helped you."

He raised his hand to get the waitress' attention. She took her time responding, finishing counting the money in the register before sauntering over with her order pad.

"What'll it be?" she asked him, turning her face to Claire and winking.

"Hamburger, no pickles, french fries and a chocolate milk shake."

"Anything else?"

Mark looked at Claire and raised his eyebrows. She shook her head. "Nope. Guess not. Seems only one of us has an appetite," he said playfully.

"More coffee, Hon?" the waitress asked Claire. Again, she shook her head and directed her gaze to the tabletop.

"You call if you need anything, O.K., Hon?"

Claire glanced up and smiled weakly. The waitress hid the side of her face closest to Mark with one hand and mouthed the word, "Cute."

Claire could feel her cheeks warm –knew she was blushing and hoped the waitress left before noticing. She looked across at Mark. The neon light from the jukebox had tinted one side of his curly brown hair a shade of pink and she almost giggled.

"Now, where did we leave off last time?" Mark then pushed back the sleeves of his sweater as if preparing for physical labor, leaned over and pulled a thick manila file from his soft-sided briefcase. After placing it on the table, he flipped through the pages to find the last entry.

"Oh, yes, we were talking about your fear of losing control." He closed the file and looked up at her with those disarming eyes. Claire reflexively touched her hair.

"Do we have to talk about that now, I mean here?" She glanced over her shoulder to check the booth behind them, but could see only the same two old men sitting at a table against the opposite wall, their hands still punctuating the finer points of what appeared to be an endless argument. The waitress was yelling at someone in the kitchen through the pick-up window.

"I mean I'm not sure I feel like talking here —it's so public." She could hear the childish whine in her voice.

"Do you mean not here, or not ever?" That was what was so maddening about Mark. He could always see right through her little attempts to avoid painful issues.

"I just mean, I just mean…"

"That you might lose control?"

"Yes," she replied softly, speaking again to the tiny gray and white dots that patterned the tabletop.

"Here you go," the waitress materialized with Mark's order, slamming it down a little loudly. "Here's the ketchup if you want it." She grabbed a bottle from another booth and set it down beside his plate.

"Be back with the coffee in a minute, Sweetie," she directed to Claire. The few moments before she returned were silent as Mark shook the bottle and squeezed the ketchup onto his plate.

"Sorry," he apologized at its rude noise. Claire tried not to giggle. How many times had her high school friends embarrassed her with that same sound, not always from the ketchup bottle? The association made her feel young and light.

"I saw it," Mark quipped, "a smile. Watch out, you might lose control."

And suddenly she did, laughing until tears ran down her cheeks, unable to stop. Everything was suddenly so funny —Mark's pink hair, the silly stern look of disapproval he was working hard to keep on his face. Even his plate, filled with food a teenager would order on a first date, beside her half empty coffee cup, seemed ridiculous. The fact that they were sitting in a diner holding a therapy session in the presence of strangers, the waitress' assumption they were lovers, the weeks she had spent alone in her tiny apartment, watching soap operas and talking only to her cat. It was all suddenly so funny…and pathetic.

Claire's body shook with convulsions as the laughter turned into deep wrenching sobs. She lay her head down on the hard table. Tears fell into pools beside her cup, but she was aware of nothing other than the violent feelings that seemed to erupt from her with the force of an uncorked geyser. She cried until her insides ached, until she had no energy left and the sobs slowly gave way to silence and an occasional catch in her throat.

"Claire?" She could hear Mark's voice but did not even have the strength to lift her head off the table.

"Claire, it's all right. I'm here." Again, she felt the pressure of his hands on her shoulder. After awhile, she could hear him sucking his milkshake through the straw —could hear him chewing and swallowing -

imagined the muscles clinching in his sharp jaw line. She heard the scrape of the plate as he pushed it away.

"Claire, look at me." She raised her head then, aware of the wetness on her cheeks and upper lip, the strands of hair stuck to her face that she didn't even try to brush away.

Rising slightly from his seat, Mark reached over with his napkin and gently wiped the skin beneath her eyes. "Now, blow," he said, bringing the napkin to her nose and holding the back of her head with his other hand the way her mother had when she was a little girl.

Only then did she notice music coming from the jukebox, the familiar voice of Andy Williams crooning the dreamy melody of her mother's favorite song, "Moon River."

Another hand touched her shoulder. "Thought a little music might help, Hon. Are you feeling better?" She looked up at the waitress' worn face, now softened with a worried smile.

"Yes, thank you," Claire whispered.

"I'll leave you two alone, then." She patted Claire's shoulder again then turned and walked quietly away.

Claire let the singer's mellow voice carry her off, rocking her gently as if she were in her mother's arms. She looked at Mark.

"You did it," he said. "You lost control. Was it so very bad, after all?" He covered her hands with his.

Claire closed her eyes so she could concentrate on the words of the old song. She waited for the last notes to die out –listened a moment to the clattering of

8

dishes in the kitchen, the low drone of the older men's voices, her own even breaths, and the slow beating of her heart. Then, she opened her eyes and gazed across the table, into the face of a man who had seen the worst, yet, was still sitting there holding her hands.

"No," she said softly. "It wasn't so bad…after all."

Chapter II

"Claire, it's time to go. I need to get back to my office for the next appointment." Mark pulled his hands away, stuffed her file back into his briefcase, and stood to leave.

Claire did not move, still somewhere far away by the bank of a wide lazy river, moonlight dancing on its surface.

"Claire," Mark said gently, "I need to leave. Do you want to stay and finish your coffee?"

She looked up then, at his face, at his eyes no longer soft and focused only on her, but ahead to his next session, his next client...probably another pathetic woman, Claire thought, suddenly overcome by an irrational jealousy.

Of course, she knew his feelings for her were purely professional, that he had spent the last hour with her out of duty, not the love she needed from someone –from some man.

"No, I'm ready." She tried to keep her voice as even as his. Before standing, she fumbled inside her purse, her now shaky hands pulling out two crumpled bills that she stuffed under the edge of the coffee saucer. She wished that she had more to leave the waitress —enough to thank her for the kindness, for the song on the jukebox, for the warm touch of the older woman's hand.

Mark grabbed his briefcase impatiently and started walking towards the door, but Claire, who seemed glued to her seat, was filled with a sudden panic, the panic she always felt when leaving anywhere- that she had forgotten something, something important and valuable. She glanced at the vinyl cushion, ran her hand down into the exposed stuffing, looked under the table at the morning's worth of crumbs and trash, at the table with Mark's empty plate and crumpled napkin, and her own half-full coffee cup. She touched the bills she had left to make sure that they were still there.

"Claire, I need to go. You have everything."

Mark's tone was definitely different. The hint of annoyance, now evident, brought a new warmth to Claire's cheeks as she forced herself to stand and turn away from the scene that only a moment before had oddly brought her so much comfort. The neon lights of the jukebox were a blur through her fresh tears.

Claire did not want the waitress to see this new distress, so trained her gaze on the dirty tile floor as Mark, who met her halfway, led her by the elbow, past the empty booths and to the door. She had not noticed when entering how smudged the glass was around the door handle, bearing the imprint of a hundred fingers and remnants of grease from the diner's food.

"You take care, Hon. Come back and see me sometime," the waitress called to Claire from her perch behind the counter.

Claire looked back quickly at the lined face, the hard mouth smiling despite the rhythmic clicking of gum.

She raised her hand limply to wave but could force no sound from her dry throat. Realizing Mark was still holding the door open, she shuffled out into the bright afternoon sun, blinded for a moment just as she had been by the dimness of the diner.

"Do you need a ride to your apartment?" Mark asked, speaking to Claire, but not, she noticed, looking into her eyes the way he had only a moment before.

Claire reached back and touched her ponytail. "No thanks, I'll walk." She gazed down at a crack in the sidewalk, ran the toe of her shoe over its edge –back and forth, back and forth -like a guilty child confessing to her parent.

"O.K., if you're sure." Mark turned abruptly and set off at a brisk pace.

"Call my secretary. I want to see you next week. I think we made progress today..." Claire could barely catch his last words, as he hurried down the sidewalk.

She studied his departing back, the familiar straight line where his hair stopped and his neck began, the way his hips swayed slightly beneath the pressed khaki pants he always wore. His leaving left a physical emptiness in her chest.

Still watching him, now so far away, dwarfed by the tall buildings on either side of the street, Claire could feel her breaths quicken, become more shallow. She rubbed her chest with one hand and shielded her eyes against the bright sun with the other, just as Mark turned the corner and disappeared.

Claire closed her eyes and could still see a negative image of his departing form, etched behind her eyelids. A sudden wave of dizziness threw her off balance and she opened her eyes, touching the brick wall behind her to keep from falling.

"Breathe, Claire," she could hear her ex-husband's voice. "Take a deep breath, blow it out." She obeyed this memory of her only child's father…the child she had born and lost moments later before the baby's tiny eyes could even open…but not before she wrapped her blue fingers around Claire's thumb as she lay on her mother's now empty belly. She clung to her mother's hand as to life, while the doctor suctioned thick mucous from her mouth and nose, then pulled her away to a corner of the dim delivery room, to massage her chest and still heart.

The doctor said later that the baby was stillborn, had never lived. But Claire bore the imprint of that elfin hand on her heart, still felt the pressure of her fingers on her own, the stubborn way they refused to open…holding on to life, to Claire.

Claire knew it was her fault that her baby had not lived. She knew that her love had not been strong enough to pull the child from the dark warmth of her womb and into the harsh light of earthly existence. It was the same light that now seemed unbearable, reflected off the dirty street and cracked sidewalk –the same light that made her close her eyes again, where Mark's image was still burned.

Claire slumped one shoulder against the wall to keep from slipping down onto the sidewalk and stayed there, willing her breaths to come evenly, deeply. "Breathe, Claire."

They had never gotten over that day, the day the baby died. David simply refused to talk about the pregnancy, the birth, their dreams of having a family. He became an automaton that jumped from the bed the minute he awoke, shaved, dressed, and went to work. In the evenings, he sat silently at the dinner table, then walked out back to the garage. Claire could hear the whir of his woodworking equipment every night until he came in to sleep beside her after a perfunctory kiss, a mere brush of lips. She didn't even know what he was building and had wondered what had become of the cradle it had taken him nine months to create.

Claire, herself, rarely spoke to David or anyone else. Her friends had retreated from the presence of so much pain. Even her sister stopped calling her, tired of the silence on the other end of the line. Claire sank deep inside herself to a world of water, like a womb –where sounds and sights were muted, distorted to a level that was bearable, that did not cause her physical pain.

That is why she didn't notice the absence of the saw's hum that night when her husband walked out after supper. Later, she didn't even notice his absence in bed. Only in the morning, in the unforgiving light of day, did she sense the emptiness beside her -which she did not mind until he came home a few days later to collect his things and tell her it was over -as though that was something she did not already know.

Claire's world had imploded after that, fallen in on itself and become smaller until all that was left were a few pieces of furniture he had not wanted, a few pictures that proved their life together had once been a reality. Claire sometimes sat up all night in her one-room apartment, her cat asleep, curled in her lap, the pressure of its weight reminding her of another weight that had briefly rested there. Her brain was so filled with unbidden images that sleep was impossible -images of their wedding, their first house, their five years of happiness before the baby's death, and, worst of all, an image of their daughter's tiny fingers clinging to her own.

A new wave of nausea swept though Claire's body and she pressed both hands against the brick wall, trying to remember where she was, how she had gotten there.

"Lady, are you all right?"

The pressure of yet another hand on her shoulder startled Claire and she stood up abruptly, her now open eyes struggling to focus in the direction of this strange voice. The image of a bearded, dirty face sharpened, and she drew her head back, hitting the wall with a thud.

"Heh, it's all right."

She could feel the man's breath on her cheek, smelling of cigarettes and something fishy.

"Do you want me to get help?"

Claire wanted to run away, willed her legs to move, but they seemed no longer connected to her brain.

"No…no, I'm…O.K. Please leave me alone." She forced her eyes to stay open, but looked down, away from the glare, away from that unpleasant face…down at the man's brown leather shoes, tied with round laces -the kind of shoes David wore to work, yet, scuffed and creased across the toes. Claire could see space around the man's ankles where they entered the shoe-tops, which even the grimy socks could not fill. He reminded Claire of a child playing dress-up with his father's clothes.

"Do you have any money?" he asked in a quiet voice.

Claire reflexively brought her purse up to her chest and held it tightly against her racing heart. At the same time, her knees weakened and she began sliding down the wall. With horror, she felt the man's hands reach under her arms to slow the descent and hugged her purse even harder.

"It's O.K.… I'm just trying to help you." The man sounded hurt. "You just sit there. Put your head down between your knees. I wasn't trying to rob you. Really. I just wondered if you had money for a taxi to take you home."

Claire could not keep back tears of panic and shame. She rested her head on her drawn-up knees, which she was hugging with all of her strength, and desperately tried to remember where she was, how she had gotten there, and if she even had a home. She searched her memory frantically for an address, any address, realizing the man was still there, leaning over, waiting for some reply. But, her mind was blank and all she could do was stare at the man's feet, too frightened to risk another look at his unkempt face, praying he would simply disappear.

Finally, she took a deep breath and, against her better judgement, forced her gaze away from the ridiculous shoes. She looked up, past the wrinkled pants, dirty shirt, two layers of sweaters beneath a long coat that was shiny with use, past the scraggly beard -and into the bluest eyes she had ever seen. The brow above was wrinkled with worry and she stared back into those eyes, saw her face reflected in them —her hair now loose and wild, her own eyes large and frightened. Something in the stranger's eyes was familiar and she suddenly remembered the waitress, the way she had winked at her, the pressure of her warm hand on Claire's shoulder.

With this memory, Claire relaxed and shifted her gaze back down to the purse pressed against her chest.

"Yes, I think I have some money...but...I can't remember where I live." She spoke not to the man, but to her knees, which were still pulled up tightly against the purse.

"Do you have a driver's license? Maybe it has your address on it."

"I don't know...I mean, I think so..." Claire struggled to clear her brain. She could see a street, a familiar street, a flight of marble stairs leading up to a large, carved wooden door. The numbers 207 hung beside the brass knocker, tarnished and dull from years of weather and neglect. If only she could remember the name of the street.

"Lady, what's wrong? Can you hear me?" The man's voice was now loud and insistent and Claire sat up straight.

"I don't want to scare you again…so, you have to look in your purse. Go ahead, open it up…"

Claire's hands obeyed his command. She opened her purse, shielding the contents from the man's stare with the top of her head. Inside, she found a wallet, the feel of the soft leather somehow familiar. She pulled it out slowly. The man took a step back then, giving her both space and light.

Claire unfolded the wallet and found a picture of a woman, a young woman, smiling and looking confidently into the camera. "I know her," she thought to herself. "Who is she?" Her mind jumped back to the moment when she had stared into the homeless man's blue eyes. She remembered the image she had seen reflected there. It looked like the woman in this picture --an older version, distorted by dark shadows under the eyes and hair that seemed out of control.

"That's me," she realized. "That's me, before… before I died," she mumbled, as if this revelation could unlock the secret of her identity.

Claire sat for a long time, studying this image of herself, wondering where that person had gone. Suddenly, the glare from the sun erased the smiling face and Claire realized the man had moved away, no longer shielding her with his shadow.

"I'll be right back...you just stay there. Don't try to get up." His words sounded wrapped in cotton to Claire. Yet, she followed his command, suddenly as trusting as a little child. She put the wallet back in her purse and rested her head on top of her knees. "207, 207," she repeated the numbers over and over again, like a mantra.

"207 South Sycamore Street! Yes, that's it, I live at 207 South Sycamore Street." The man had just returned. She spoke the address over and over to him, her voice becoming louder and nearing hysteria with each repetition.

"You hear that, Joe? She lives at 207 South Sycamore." He pulled her gently to her feet, then led her slowly towards a yellow cab parked at the curb. He waited until she was safely seated inside, then leaned in before closing the door.

"You take care, m'lady. Go home and lie down. Eat something. You're too skinny...pretty, but too skinny."

Claire looked up, into the kind blue eyes of this stranger, wanting to thank him, but, not knowing what words to say. He winked, then closed the car door, stepped back from the curb and bent forward in an exaggerated bow complete with a flourish of his half-gloved hand.

"Take good care of her, Joe."

"Sure thing," the driver grunted as he drove away from the curb. Claire turned and looked back through the dirty windshield...saw the man still standing there, waving, almost lost in his heavy coat and big shoes.

"You're skinny, pretty, but too skinny." When had anyone ever told her she was pretty? Had he really called her "m'lady?"

Thinking of those kind words and the stranger's refined voice which contrasted comically with his clown-like appearance, Claire smoothed the wild wisps of hair back and retied her ponytail, and for the second time that day, smiled.

Chapter III

Claire did not recognize any of the buildings or shops they passed after leaving the diner. Ordinarily, that would have engendered a new state of panic, but Claire felt calm and safe inside the cab. Occasionally, she studied the back of Joe's head –his hairline, unlike Mark's, dipped down to a central point on his neck, which Claire could barely make out through the stray strands that brushed the collar of his light blue shirt. She could see only his eyes in the rearview mirror, not his whole face...could not make out their color, but noted the lines at their corners slanted upward, and knew whoever this "Joe" was, he laughed a lot.

"You feeling better?" he called to her over his shoulder.

"Oh yes, much better," she said with a confidence that surprised her. They settled into a comfortable silence. Claire gazed out the window at the people on the sidewalk -studied their faces, made up stories about their lives, their professions, where they were headed with such resolute purpose. She searched for signs of distress or doubt and found none that resembled her own usual state of angst that she dragged behind her like a ball and chain.

Some were even smiling, lips pursed as if whistling a tune. "Why can't I simply live in the moment, moving forward to some clear destination, not always sucked under by the past of 'what if's' and 'why's?' What is wrong with me?" she silently berated herself.

Claire was so engrossed in this mental flagellation that she failed to notice the cab had stopped moving.

"Here we are –207 South Sycamore," the cabby called back a little too loudly and Claire guiltily wondered if he were repeating it for the second time. Glancing quickly out her window, she was relieved to see the familiar worn marble steps leading up to the door of her apartment house.

She fumbled in her purse for money to pay the fare but came up with exactly thirty-seven cents.

"I'm…I'm sorry. I don't seem to have much money. If you could wait a minute, I'll go inside and get more." There was no answer from the front and Claire realized the driver had gotten out and was walking around to open her door.

"Let me help you, m'lady," the driver spoke in a fairly believable Cockney accent as he reached a hand in to assist Claire out of the vehicle.

"M'lady is not to worry about the fare as it was already taken care of by her kind friend, the honorable Duke of Danvers Street."

"Who?" She shook her head in bewilderment, and like a magic 8 ball, the motion brought a picture to the surface of a bearded face and two bright blue eyes. "Oh…I remember now."

Claire decided to play along with the driver's theatrics, and, once on the sidewalk, turned and curtseyed, attempting to mimic an upper-class British accent.

"Please tell the Duke that his kindness is greatly appreciated."

The driver, still holding her hand, nodded.

"Good day, m'lady." He bowed and spoke with such a stern tone and straight face that Claire could not hold back a giggle, at which cue, the driver's face split open with a wide smile. He bowed again, shut her door and walked stiffly around the cab and slid into his seat.

As he pulled away, he gave a final tip of his hat which Claire answered with the royal wave she had seen on a documentary of Queen Elizabeth: fingers pointed up, slightly bent, hand rotating delicately from side to side.

Claire stood at the curb until the cab was out of sight, unaware of people walking past on either side, giving her a wide berth. One woman turned to stare at this strange young person still waving her hand limply, apparently at no one.

So caught up in this Elizabethan fantasy, Claire might have stood there longer if a man, dressed in a gray business suit and carrying a briefcase similar to Mark's, had not inadvertently knocked into her.

"Sorry," he said not stopping his forward thrust.

"Oh, that's O.K." Claire realized he could not hear her —one hand held to his ear.

"No, no, I said the meeting with the investors is at four. What? Can you hear me? We seem to be breaking up…" His words faded with the phone signal. Claire watched him walk away, noted a dark spot on his shirt collar, sweat glistening on his neck below the hairline. He was obviously rushing off to a world different from Claire's –a world of buy-outs and sell-offs, designer suits and $100 hair cuts, shirts laundered expertly to remove the success-induced sweat.

She followed his shrinking form until it, too, disappeared around a corner and then brought her gaze back down to her feet, to the sidewalk with its familiar cracks, one of which led to the base of the marble stairs, the dazzling sunlight masking its own cracks and dingy corners.

"I'm home," she mumbled, as she placed a foot on the first step. It took such effort to bend her knee and pull the other foot up to the second step that she grabbed onto the side railing. Its worn smoothness felt soothing, and she was suddenly overcome by a desperate need to reach the top, push open the heavy wooden door and collapse into the dark stale air of the hallway. Once there, closing the door behind her, Claire stood still for a moment, allowing her eyes to adjust to the sudden dimness, breathing in slowly the stagnant air, which was heavy with the odor of frying bacon.

It was a smell she associated with early mornings in her childhood home when she had lain in her bed, wrapped in her butterfly print comforter. Inside her cocoon, she had felt safe from her parent's unhappiness, or rather, their individual unhappiness that translated into seemingly endless arguments that she could hear through the thin wall that separated their bedroom from hers.

Some nights, Claire could make out her father's words, followed by what sounded like a woman's moan or low muffled sob. Once, she thought she had heard him speak her name in the midst of what had become a familiar diatribe.

"Mary, I work my fingers to the bone while you sit around all day doing God knows what. All I ask is a little peace and quiet —a little respect from you and our daughter...I'm sick and tired of dealing with her, with her ee-mo-tion-al problems...and as for you..."

"Cal, shush..." At that, they had lowered their voices, though Claire could still hear the rise and fall of the angry tones which she could only erase by wrapping her comforter around her head and burrowing deeper into her tear-soaked pillow.

Each morning, after the ugly scene of the night before, her mother rose early, went downstairs to start the coffee and fry bacon for her husband's breakfast. By the time Claire found the nerve to dress and go downstairs, Mary would be standing in a thin cotton robe before the stove, usually humming a soft tune as she turned the strips of bacon. Her father would be dressed as usual in shirts her mother spent hours washing, starching, and ironing...his tie perfectly knotted at his throat, his suit coat hung carefully on the back of the kitchen chair. Cal was usually too absorbed in the business section of the paper to notice Claire's entrance, as she tiptoed across the linoleum floor and slid noiselessly into her place at the neatly set table.

Her mother, still turned toward her task, would call over her shoulder in a cheerful voice, "Morning sweetie. Want some eggs?" Not waiting for Claire's reply, she would resume humming her tune, usually something soft and dreamy.

"Will you please cut out that racket? How's a person supposed to think with all that noise?" her father barked, as if on cue. Still not turning around, Mary's song would abruptly stop. Despite a slight droop of her shoulders and without missing a beat, she would fill two plates with eggs, bacon, and perfectly browned toast, then turn with a cheery smile and place her morning offering on the family's Formica altar.

Once, Claire thought she saw a tear slide down Mary's cheek and onto her unbuttered toast. But, her father did not seem to notice and after he had finished his meal, he wordlessly donned his jacket, brushed her mother's wet cheek lightly with his lips, and tousled Claire's carefully brushed hair before walking out the door.

The morning Claire saw the tear, she summoned the nerve to ask her mother if everything was all right.

"Of course, sweetie. Why wouldn't it be?" Mary assured her in what Claire knew was forced cheerfulness. Once, just once, she would have liked her mother to be honest, let Claire know her real feelings. How could she possibly think Claire didn't know the truth? No amount of bright smiles and cheery reassurances could mute the memory of the ugly words Claire heard every night through the bedroom wall.

Claire knew her father was to blame, running the household like a tyrant. But, she secretly despised her mother for not standing up to him, for not admitting something was wrong, merely perpetuating this "Ozzie and Harriet" charade for Claire's sake.

"I will never let a man do that to me," Claire had vowed one night when the noise was particularly brutal.

And, yet, hadn't she behaved exactly like her mother in her own marriage to David after the baby's death? Hadn't she gone through the motions of each day's carefully set pattern, pushing down her grief and anger –keeping silent as her husband drifted farther away, finally fading from her life like the sugar he stirred nightly into his iced tea?

A door-slam upstairs brought Claire back to the moment. She did not know how long she had been standing in the hall, but could tell by the change in the slant of light through the windows on either side of the door, that it had been more than just a few minutes.

Her eyes now accustomed to the dimness, she walked to the back of the corridor, guided by a swatch of sunlight beaming in from the window. Once there, she searched inside her purse for the keys. Forgetting which one opened the apartment door, or the purpose of any of the keys, she asked out loud, "Why do I have so many?" Trying to keep from panicking, she decided to be systematic and try each key one at a time. Luckily, the second entered the keyhole smoothly and she heard the tumblers click as she turned the handle and pushed the door open.

The inside of her apartment was as dark as the hall. Claire walked quickly to each of the three windows and drew up the off-white mini-blinds her sister's husband had installed for her when she moved in last winter. Most of the time, Claire kept the blinds drawn and closed, both to shut out the light which sometimes hurt her eyes and to keep heat from the old radiator from escaping. But, if she were honest, she would admit she kept them drawn to shut out the world and encircle herself in four solid walls —a fortress strong enough to contain her bed, TV, table, single chair, her cat —and her pain.

Claire was shocked to see how dusty everything appeared once bathed in the light. Thousands of dust motes danced in the streaks of sunlight beaming in on the stacks of books and old papers on the table, and the pile of food-encrusted dishes overflowing in the sink. As Claire stood in the middle of the room, turning slowly as if seeing all these familiar objects for the first time, her cat, Max, walked in circles around her legs. He rubbed his body and muzzle against her pants, meowing softly but insistently as he tried to push her towards his empty food bowl.

Claire's shoe caught the edge of the old china saucer that clattered noisily across the wooden floor. She bent down to pick up her indignant kitty, rubbing his ears and head and crooning, "Oh, you poor baby. Mommy forgot —bad, bad, Mommy." Still carrying Max under one arm, Claire walked the few steps to the kitchen and opened the refrigerator.

"Now, that's just pathetic," she told Max. The shelves held a plate containing a hunk of dried cheese, green mold dotting one end, a half-eaten TV dinner, two containers of yogurt, and an opened can of cat food. Claire had forgotten to cover the latter with plastic wrap and the chilled smell of spoiled fish wafted out, nearly causing her to gag. Still holding Max, she managed to pick up the can with two fingers and shut the refrigerator door quickly. To catch her breath, Claire leaned against the closed door, holding the can as far from her nose as possible.

"I can't give this to my sweet kitty," she spoke to the cat as she would to a human baby, and tossed the offending food into the trashcan that stood beside the refrigerator. The tin hit the bottom with a hollow "thunk," and Claire realized that she had forgotten to install a plastic liner. Hoping an additional door would further isolate the unpleasant smell, Claire quickly grabbed the container and slid it into the cabinet beneath the sink.

Straightening up with some difficulty, she then reached overhead to search the sticky shelf above the stove where she kept canned goods. The first item her hand touched proved to be a can of tomato soup, the next a nearly empty jar of peanut butter. Rising onto her tiptoes, she felt all the way to the back of the cabinet, but with no luck.

Claire stood for a moment, resting her back against the edge of the sink, pondering this new problem.

Her first and usual impulse at such times was to indulge in heavy bouts of self-recrimination. She was responsible for only one other living thing –a being totally dependent on her care for its survival –and here she failed even him. Perhaps, the baby was better off dead, she mused, than to be stuck with such a forgetful, irresponsible mother.

"Poor Max," Claire mumbled. He would starve unless she could find the change at the bottom of her purse. But that would require going out again, walking the two blocks to Dulaney's Market, risking being seen, or worse, forced to talk to someone –another stranger, perhaps, or Dulaney's wife who always managed to work some belittling insult into Claire's simplest request for assistance.

She felt defeated –did not even have the strength to hold onto her squirming cat. Max escaped with a thud, landing on the kitchen floor where he resumed his circular siege of his mistress' legs. Claire was aware of his piteous cries, but was too exhausted to even think about leaving her apartment, her refuge. She also knew she would get no peace that night unless she satisfied Max' hunger and reached down to open the door under the sink. Holding her breath, she carefully retrieved the opened tin from the bottom of the trash can, noting with disgust that some of its contents had spilled out onto the bottom of the bin. Claire promised Max that she would deal with the mess later. But, his only concern appeared to be filling his empty stomach, and he began meowing so loudly that Claire was afraid he would disturb her elderly neighbor.

"Animals can eat garbage. They have stronger stomachs than humans," she reasoned, as she scraped the last bits of meat onto Max' dish. Holding the can at arms length, she retreated quickly to the sink, opened the door a crack so she could toss the can inside, then slammed the cabinet shut.

Afraid the noise had startled Max, Claire turned around just in time to see her cat walk daintily over to his dish. He sniffed the contents only once, then pivoted gracefully, walking off with his fluffy tail sticking straight up, backside aimed towards Claire in an obvious act of disgust.

Claire sighed, stood for a moment more, reviewing the bright room and its dusty contents, then moved to each window, roughly closing the blinds against the afternoon sun. She collapsed into the single bed that substituted as a couch and sank the weight of her back and head into the large pillows propped up against the wall. Max jumped up into her lap, kneaded her thighs with his strong paws, then circled several times before settling down for a nap. Ignoring the pinpricks of pain, Claire stroked his head, then reached back to pull the rubber band from her ponytail, letting her hair escape wildly. Soon, the quiet of the room was replaced with the purr of a contented feline, and Claire marveled that her cat still seemed to love her, despite her many failings.

For a long time, she did not move, except for the hand sliding across his soft fur, her eyes fixed hypnotically on the white and marmalade stripes. Claire felt weak and spent, energy draining from every pore in her body and sinking down into the bedclothes, just like the frequent nights when she woke shivering, her pajamas soaked with sweat.

She closed her eyes, let her thoughts float away one by one to the rhythm of Max' motor —watched them bob up and down on the surface of an imaginary river then disappear around the bend. She began to hum the song that she had heard earlier at the diner -until the river, itself, seemed to stop its flow and she sank down to its muddy bottom into her safe dark world.

Chapter IV

A persistent knocking pulled Claire back up to the surface. Reluctantly, she opened one eye wide enough to see that it was still light outside. She closed it again to shut out the glare and had just begun to sink back into sleep when the knocking, louder now, broke through her stupor.

"Claire, open the door. It's me!" Claire recognized her sister's voice. "I know you are in there —open the door!"

Both eyes open now, Claire sat up. A sharp pain at the nape of her neck kept her from raising her head completely. She couldn't have been sleeping for long, yet, every joint and muscle rebelled against her will to move. The front of her thighs ached with cold —the spot where Max usually rested.

Panic brought Claire to the edge of the bed, the pain of the sudden movement dulled by her fear—the knocking still only an annoyance, like the buzz of a mosquito in her ear.

"Max," she called out. "Max, where are you?"

Claire stood up suddenly, the blood rushed to her feet leaving her head light and empty. Tiny sparks danced before her eyes. Afraid she would fall, she reached out blindly for the edge of the table and held onto it until her vision cleared.

"Max!" Her voice was high and shrill.

"Claire, open the door!" Her sister's voice, too, was edged with alarm, her words still no more than white noise devoid of meaning to Claire.

Her vision still blurred, Claire closed her eyes and forced herself to breathe –in and out, in and out –until she could feel her heart rate slowing down. When she opened them, the front windows came into focus, bright morning light pushing past the drawn blinds. Just above the sill of the middle window, the blinds bulged out and Claire could see a dark form silhouetted against the slats. Her arms and legs weak with relief, she hurried across the room and yanked the cord that hung to the right of the window frame.

The sudden glare brought a new pain, this time deep inside her brain, behind her eyes, and she winced, shutting her eyelids reflexively. Desperately, she reached towards the windowsill and grabbed the sun-warmed fur on Max' back.

"Max, Max, you naughty boy. You scared Mommy. Come here." She picked him up, his body hanging limply across one arm, hard to hold onto as if it contained no bones.

Claire buried her face in his fur, sniffed his carefully cleaned body, chastising him softly as she would a naughty child.

"O.K., Claire, I hear you in there. If you don't open the door now, I'm going to get the landlord."

Claire's brain suddenly interpreted the noise from the hallway as words. Still clutching Max, she shuffled the few steps to the door and unlatched the dead bolt.

Her sister fell into the apartment, pushing Claire and Max backwards onto the bed. Claire instinctively curled herself around Max, cringing to shield herself from what she knew would be her sister's angry words.

Born ten years before Claire and already married when her younger sister was in third grade, Nita had always seemed more like a mother than a sibling. Even though, now, they were both adults, Claire still felt like a little girl in her presence, the same little girl that cried herself to sleep when Nita refused to let her have a nightlight.

"You are not a baby any longer…you're just spoiled!" Nita would snap at her before closing the bedroom door, blocking out the comforting light coming up the stairs from the living room. Claire looked forward to her sister's visits on those weekends when her husband had to work, but dreaded the nights when their parents went out, leaving Nita to baby sit.

Claire hugged Max tightly, then risked raising her eyes enough to look up at Nita's imposing form, silhouetted by the light of the window. She was standing just as she had in the doorway of Claire's bedroom - legs apart, hands in a fist firmly planted on each hip, muscles tensed like a bull about to be let out of the gate.

"Claire, why didn't you answer the door? I'd been out there for fifteen minutes. What were you doing?"

"I was just taking a nap," Claire replied in her small child's voice.

"A nap in the middle of the morning? Are you sick?" Immediately, Nita's voice softened with maternal concern and she reached across, placing the palm of her hand on Claire's forehead, its warmth and softness easing the pain that still pulsed behind Claire's eyes.

"No fever." Nita withdrew her hand, though Claire could still feel its pressure. "Claire, honey, I got worried last night when you didn't call. Where were you?"

Claire was too disoriented to reply. Apparently, she had slept through the night and the brightness that was still bothering her eyes came from the morning sun of another day. Claire knew she had disappointed her big sister…again. She quickly scanned Nita's face, searching for any signs of disgust, and was relieved to find nothing but worry reflected on the smooth skin.

Nita was only a few inches taller than Claire. She was not fat, but large boned, and well padded in all the places Claire wasn't. "My Earthmother," Claire often called Nita in her sessions with Mark, referring not only to her sister's green thumb with flowers and vegetables, but also to how safe she felt in Nita's soft embrace.

Nita's hair was dark like Claire's, but worn short. She had it trimmed every six weeks so that it never seemed to grow. It was more like a wig in its consistent neatness, so unlike Claire's wild curls that could only be controlled by pulling them back into a tight ponytail. Nita had more than once suggested that Claire have her hair cut, had offered to make an appointment with her stylist and had offered to pay for it when Claire protested at the expense. Claire had refused, not just out of shame for being poor, but to hold onto some sense of herself that had survived the baby's death, the divorce, and the bouts of depression.

Motherhood had come so easily to Nita. Married to her childhood sweetheart just after high school graduation, Nita had born her first child two years later, after only three hours of labor. Two more children came along within the next three years, so that, for a time, she was either constantly nursing or pregnant or both. When her two oldest children left for college, Nita channeled all that maternal energy into a volunteer job at a local hospital rocking premature babies. She would sit for hours with her tiny charges, nestled against her ample breasts and soft belly, singing to them softly until they were strong enough to go home. So far, Nita had not lost even one baby and had become somewhat of a local celebrity when the paper featured her in an article about the positive effects of physical nurture on the survival of at-risk infants.

Nita had been very supportive right after Claire and David lost their baby –had held Claire for hours, rocking her while she cried. But even she had lost patience, when after months had passed, Claire still grieved as though her loss was fresh. Nita had become tired of calling Claire and waiting minutes for her sister to reply to the simplest question.

"You'll get over this, Sis," Nita told Claire. "You're young. You and David can try again." But none of the comforting words had penetrated the thick wall of

Claire's sorrow. She was too ashamed to admit to Nita that she and David had never again made love.

Nita had stayed with Claire for a few nights after David came home, for the last time, to retrieve his clothes. She had held Claire again, rocked her, whispered reasoning words such as, "You'll be your old self in no time, Sis. You'll meet someone else and have a family." Nita finally gave up trying to pull Claire from her deep world -decided she must like it there -and had left a few nights later in disgust and defeat.

When David called to say he was selling the house, Nita drove Claire around the city to look for a suitable apartment in a safe, respectable neighborhood. The task had proved difficult, since the choices were limited to places Claire could afford with her monthly alimony, having chosen to abandon her teaching job after the baby's death. She viewed each place with the same disinterest and listlessness, until they'd found this apartment. Nita thought the building was shabby, despite its uptown address, but Claire had fallen in love with the single room –it's three large windows and bathroom no bigger than a closet.

Grateful that Claire could show feeling for anything, Nita had acquiesced and she and her husband, Fred, a cabinetmaker by trade, had moved Claire's few pieces of furniture and meager possessions to the apartment. It had taken only one load in Fred's pick-up truck to empty the house of any trace of Claire and David's five years of residence.

Claire had waited for them at the empty apartment, having said her good-byes to the house a few weeks before when she moved in with Nita and Fred. She did not want to go there again…knew she would be drawn to the room upstairs decorated with clouds that she had painted on the light blue walls and iridescent stars on the ceiling. She could not bear to see the curtains that still covered the single window, made from a fabric filled with bright rainbows. She could not bear to see the rocking chair David had made from the same wood he used to build the cradle. Claire had found both of his projects in a corner of the garage, carefully wrapped in a canvas drop cloth.

"Claire, look at me." Nita's voice sounded like Mark's —sharp, but with edges muted by concern. Nita sat in the single chair facing Claire, close enough to rest her hands on her younger sister's knees, warming the legs which once again ached with cold and emptiness. Max had wriggled free to sunbathe in the window.

Claire sighed deeply, then slowly looked at her sister's face, fascinated with the lack of lines around Nita's eyes or anywhere on her face, for that matter. Nita's physical abundance and perpetual optimism seemed to defy the laws of aging and Claire envied her sister's ability to attack a problem with the certainty that she would find a solution.

"That's better…stay with me," Nita encouraged. "God, Sis, you look awful. Have you had breakfast? I bet you slept in your clothes again, didn't you?"

Unable to answer or comprehend two questions at once, her mind still standing at the edge of the watery world of unconsciousness, the only place she felt at peace, Claire started to close her eyes.

"You're not leaving me, again, little Sis."

Claire recognized the tone of Nita's voice –the tone she had used when Claire had misbehaved on the nights their parents were away. It had both frightened and comforted her as a child. Nita had always been the rock on which Claire could cling while the stormy waters of their parent's misery swirled around them. She forced herself to obey, though her eyelids felt heavy.

"Now, sit up straight and take some deep breaths. Breathe in, out, in, out...Good!" Nita took her hands away from Claire's thighs slowly, keeping them on either side of Claire's body in case her sister tried to lie down again.

"I'm going to make some coffee. Where do you keep it?" Nita rose and took two steps to the tiny kitchen, turning around when Claire made no response.

"Claire, where do you keep the coffee?" She spoke loudly, pronouncing each syllable carefully, as she would to a deaf person who could read lips.

Claire, now fully awake, sat rubbing her stiff arms and neck.

"I don't have any coffee. I ran out a couple of days ago, I think," she admitted. "Guess I haven't had a chance to go to the store."

Before Claire could finish her last sentence, Nita started opening each cabinet, slamming the doors shut. She curled her nose at the odor that emanated from the space under the sink. Opening the refrigerator last, she clicked her tongue in disapproval at its scant contents.

"No wonder you look half dead," she faced her sister in that familiar two-fisted stance. "Come on, Sis, brush your hair. I'm taking you to get a decent breakfast, then to the store. No arguments!" Nita stomped into the bathroom, returning moments later with a steaming wash cloth and Claire's matted brush.

"Here, wipe your face. I don't see how you could use this thing," Nita remonstrated as she yanked a month's worth of Claire's dark hair from the bristles, tossing it under the sink quickly before the fish odor could escape.

"I don't know why you won't get this mess cut off." Nita knelt on the bed beside Claire, pulling the brush through the tangles, gently at first, then, losing patience, tugging with such force that tears stung Claire's eyes, though she did not protest.

Nita brushed the curls back from Claire's forehead, clearing her brow. Claire suddenly felt light, as if a weight had been lifted from her head and her eyes opened wider than they had for days.

"Give me that thing." Nita motioned towards Claire's wrist. Obeying her sister, Claire slipped the rubber band off of her wrist, then rubbed the sore indentation it left behind. Nita smoothed her sister's hair back with her hands, pulling it up into a high ponytail, then coiling the ends around into a tight bun. She stepped back to survey her work.

"Now, that's a definite improvement. Go see." She nodded her head in satisfaction, then motioned towards the bathroom.

The skin on Claire's face and forehead was so taut, she could not move her mouth to answer. She rose slowly, holding her head as still as a newly crowned prom queen afraid of losing her tiara, and walked into the bathroom. Claire stood at the sink, gazing down at the spots of soap scum and dried toothpaste, reluctant to raise her head to the mirror.

"Go on, look. You're gorgeous!" Nita stood in the doorway. Claire could feel the physical force of her older sister's will and, resigned, brought her eyes up to the medicine cabinet that hung above the sink.

The image reflected back was vaguely familiar –the mouth and chin definitely, perhaps the nose. But, the eyes were those of a stranger –eyebrows pulled up and arched, eyes round and fully opened. Claire stood for a moment, the features of her face blurring as she focused on the outline of her jaw and ears, the shape of her head. New features filled the void inside the outline and she gasped, grabbing the edges of the sink to keep from falling.

Nita reached over quickly to support Claire under one arm. "What is it, sweetie? Are you O.K.? Don't you like the way I fixed your hair?" Nita's voice was softer now.

"Oh…yes," Claire answered faintly. "I thought I saw…" Claire gulped, tried to swallow and push down the bile that had risen in her throat. "I never noticed how much I look like Dad."

"You didn't used to, I mean, when you had some meat on your bones." Nita smoothed back a single wisp of hair that had freed itself from the neat bun. "I see it, too, now that your face is so thin. But, he was a handsome man, a mean son of a bitch, but handsome. Don't you remember how women used to stare at him when we walked in the park on Sunday afternoons? He loved it, too —always turned to smile and nod at them. Mother hated it, of course, not that he was handsome, but that he seemed to enjoy other women's attention a little too much…"

"I don't want to talk about him!" Claire pushed past Nita with surprising strength, at the same time pulling the rubber band violently from her head. Nita could hear her sister's hair tear as she shook the tangled strands free.

"I'm ready —let's go." Claire pulled her hair back and secured it in a ponytail at the nape of her neck, then grabbed her jacket from under one of the bed pillows, ramming her arms into the sleeves before Nita could react.

"But, your clothes. You need to at least change your clothes."

"Let's go…Now!" Claire spoke with such force Nita was momentarily speechless. "Now!"

Nita closed her mouth and grabbed her purse from the table, hurrying after her sister who was already out the door and halfway down the dark hall.

Before pulling the apartment door closed behind her, Nita called to Claire, "Do you have your keys?" Claire was already outside and down the steps to the sidewalk and could not hear her sister's question.

Worried she might lose Claire again, Nita pulled the door shut, rushing down the tight corridor with the innate grace of someone at home in her body. Claire was standing at the base of the steps, her back to the rail, but not leaning on it.

"O.K., Claire, I'm coming." Nita spoke in what she hoped was a soothing tone, not wanting to startle this wounded animal, afraid she might run headlong into the street.

As she eased down the steps, Nita studied the back of Claire's head, the untidy ponytail spilling down her back. She was grateful for this new sign of life in her sister, but wary lest it should prove short-lived or, worse, a sign of mania. Moving as noiselessly as possible, she stopped at the last step just as Claire turned her head. Their eyes met and, for the first time in months, Nita saw another human soul looking back.

Chapter V

Half an hour later, Claire and Nita sat across from each other at a small table. Since Claire had voiced no opinion when asked, Nita had steered her to a coffee shop a few blocks from Claire's apartment. Their table was pushed up against the large plate-glass front window. The morning sun slanted sideways across the polished wooden top, gleaming off the stainless steel salt-and-peppershakers.

Claire would have preferred a table in the back of the restaurant. But Nita, who ardently believed in the benefits of frequent exposure to bright light, had pulled her sister gently by the arm and pushed her into the seat facing the side wall. The sun-warmed chair felt soothing to Claire's tired back, but the glare made her wish she had remembered her purse where she kept a pair of darkly tinted sunglasses. Nita sat in the shade, oblivious to Claire's discomfort, stuffing pieces of almond croissant into her mouth between sips of a large caramel cappuccino.

Claire had not wanted anything to eat, just ordered black coffee that turned out to be so bitter she could only take small sips. Nita, however, had insisted she eat something and had purchased a bran muffin, loaded with nuts and dried fruit. The muffin now sat on a napkin in front of Claire, shredded into ragged pieces. Only a few of the crumbs, Nita noticed, actually made it to Claire's lips.

It was a trick Claire had perfected as an anorexic teenager to fool her parents into thinking she had eaten more than just a few nibbles of her dinner. She had become expert at cutting the meat and vegetables into tiny pieces, stabbing them with her fork and sliding them around on the plate. Every so often, she would bring the empty fork to her mouth, chewing and swallowing nothing but air.

The subterfuge had worked for awhile, until one night, when she left to visit a friend before clearing the table, her usual job. Her mother noticed when taking Claire's plate to the kitchen that it seemed the same weight as when she had placed it in front of her seemingly cheerful, almost giddy daughter.

From then on, her parents watched her closely at each meal, forced Claire to eat everything on her plate before leaving the table. Claire had complied, heading straight to the bathroom to purge every bite afterwards.

Claire found other ways of hiding her disorder from her parents, though she did not consider her pattern of starvation, bingeing, and purging, an illness. She delighted each time she stepped on the scales and had lost a pound, looked at her naked body for hours in the full-length mirror her father had hung on the back of the closet door. In her eyes, she saw a beautiful model looking back, instead of the ghastly skeleton she had become.

Loose, baggy clothing hid her protruding bones from her parents, who assumed she was getting enough nutrition at their regimented meals. Claire had not told her mother that her periods had stopped, nor that she often had to sit out the second half of dance class, too weak and out of breath to continue.

In gym class, complaining of constant cold, she had been allowed to wear sweat clothes over her gym suit. Each day, she changed from her school clothes inside a locked toilet stall, not wanting to expose her secret to the criticism of her so-called friends. She knew they would be jealous of her newly achieved beauty.

But one day, during a game of volleyball, Claire had fainted. The school nurse called Claire's mother to pick her up and, when she did, urged her to take her daughter directly to the doctor's office.

"She's awfully thin, Mrs. Roberts. Did she eat breakfast this morning?" she asked Mary.

"Claire eats breakfast every day. I don't let her out the door without something warm in her stomach, something that will stick to her ribs," her mother had replied defensively.

The nurse's question planted a seed of doubt in Mary's mind. She began to notice how Claire always went to the bathroom after each meal, closing and locking the door, then flushing the toilet several times. When she confronted Claire, her daughter had reacted angrily.

"Don't I have a right to privacy in my own house?" Claire had screamed. "You and Daddy just don't trust me. You think I'm still a little girl!"

Mary watched in horror as her normally obedient and soft-spoken child, ran up the stairs, slamming her bedroom door behind her.

The next day, she had taken Claire to the family doctor. Her daughter had insisted on being weighed still wearing her heavy shoes and winter coat. Even so, the scales barely touched 100 pounds, well below the recommended weight for a growing girl who had already reached the height of 5'6".

Mary had been shocked by her daughter's weight, became defensive again when the doctor, an older man who had been their family physician since Nita was a baby, questioned her about Claire's eating habits.

"I'm not exactly sure what's wrong with her, Mrs. Roberts. Is she getting enough to eat? I know it's tough to get teenagers to eat anything except junk food."

Mary replied with the same indignant response she had used in the school clinic.

"Well, there may be a problem with her thyroid," the doctor suggested, more to calm the woman than out of conviction. "She looks anemic. I'll send my nurse in to draw some blood. I'll call you in a few days with the results. Meanwhile, try to get her to eat a well balanced diet…plenty of protein, vegetables and fruit."

He left the room abruptly. Mary felt more angry at his insinuations that she was not a good parent, than she was alarmed about Claire's fragile physical state.

Once alone with her daughter, she had grabbed her by the shoulders.

"How could you do this to us? Your father works hard to provide for his family, and I put a lot of time and effort into preparing good nutritious meals. Your sister never had any trouble eating what I cooked."

Mary paused a moment to catch her breath and waited for her daughter's response. Claire sat on the examining table, staring straight ahead, her face expressionless. She had stopped listening during the doctor's exam, had paid no attention to his or her mother's words, feeling her presence in the room at all was superfluous. Instead, she heard her father's voice, remembered something he had said to her one night at dinner, a few years ago, when her breasts had begun to grow and her hips become round.

"You'd better be careful, Claire," Cal had said. "You don't want to get fat like..." He directed his gaze to Claire's mother whose body had broadened as a result of two pregnancies and the inevitable extra pounds of middle age. Later that same night, he had teased Claire as she sat eating ice cream while watching a TV sitcom. "You know, ice cream was your mother's downfall. I can see you're taking after her."

Another night at dinner, her parents discussed their neighbor whose husband had recently left her for a younger woman. "I can't blame him," her father had said. "Who would want to spend the rest of their life with that fat cow?"

"Claire, are you listening to me?" Mary asked as she pulled the car into the driveway that led to their two-story brick house on a quiet suburban street.

Claire could not remember having left the doctor's office. She was too exhausted to answer her mother. Once inside, she climbed the stairs to her bedroom, locked the door behind her, and collapsed onto the bed. Several hours later, she woke shivering from the cold. She could hear her parents arguing loudly on the other side of the wall. She wrapped herself tightly in her comforter, then willed herself to sleep.

The next day, Claire stayed in her room, refusing to open the door or answer her father's demand that she let him in. That night, after coming home from work and finding his daughter still barricaded in her room, he had broken the lock, pushing his way into her sanctuary.

"Get up," Cal had ordered in the low rumble of a volcano about to explode. He stood beside her bed, not saying another word, until Claire, frightened by his quick, ragged breathing, crawled out from under the covers. Her knees trembled when she tried to stand.

"Take off your clothes," her father demanded. When Claire made no effort to move, he began pulling her shirt up over her head, wrenching it free from her head and arms. He unbuttoned the top of her jeans, then yanked them down around her knees. Claire was so shocked she didn't even have time to shield her breasts from his stare.

"My God, what have you done to yourself?" The sight of her emaciated body literally threw him off-balance and he stepped back, his eyes boring holes through the thin skin that covered her chest and jutting pubic bones. "You used to be so pretty…now you look like a boy."

As if her mind were detached from her body, Claire watched her father's red face as it turned a shade of green and wondered if his deep swallows would keep him from vomiting all over her bed.

"Put some clothes on. I don't want to look at you." Cal grabbed another pair of jeans from the chair beside the bed and a wrinkled tee shirt from the top dresser drawer. Claire stood perfectly still, paralyzed with horror at her father's words. She was still somewhat disconnected from this terrible scene, yet, his anger penetrated the emotional fog and left her feeling violated and vulnerable. She obeyed his command, but with a catatonic compliance. Impatient with her slowness, he began to dress her as he had often done when she was a little girl. The touch of his rough hands felt almost like a caress through the cotton in which her mind was now wrapped.

Without warning, he grabbed her arm, dragged her across the room, opened the closet door, and pushed her inside. Claire heard the sickening click of the lock after he closed the door.

"You just stay in there and think about what you've done to yourself…to us." Her father had never spoken to her in that tone, the one she heard through the wall at night.

The darkness in the closet was complete, save for the tiny strip of light at the base of the door. Claire, stunned at first, began banging on the closed door, begging to be let out, promising to be good and do everything her parents said. Her cries were met with silence.

Finally, exhausted, her eyes nearly swollen shut with crying, she slid down onto the closet floor where she curled herself into a tight ball. She was oblivious of the sharp edges of shoes and boxes that poked her bottom and back. She was oblivious of the fading light that became the complete darkness of a tomb. For she was already in her own wet, dark world…where she felt safe and loved.

The drugs Claire was given at the hospital stole days and weeks from her memory. She couldn't even remember how she had gotten there.

Claire followed the doctors' and nurses' orders, did not resist the needle pricks, stepped willingly on the scales when asked, ate every bite of the bland food. She attended every group therapy session, speaking only in short syllables when asked a question, never initiating conversation with her fellow inmates. Most were girls her age, in varying stages of malnutrition, all with the same hollow eyes and dry brittle hair. Some were agitated and violent at times or cried incessantly, like her roommate, a tiny girl who sobbed nightly after the nurse turned out their light. Claire could see her curled into a fetal position on the narrow bed, illuminated by the light from the hallway, but never tried to comfort her or seek out the source of her deep unhappiness.

Five weeks to the day after her father brought her to the institution, he and her mother had come to pick her up. They stood in her room as she packed her toiletries and stuffed her comforter into the canvas duffel bag her father had brought a few days after she was admitted.

"Claire has made a lot of progress, gained nine pounds. I think with careful supervision, we can treat her as an outpatient. She's definitely not as medically at-risk as when she arrived," the facility's doctor had explained to her parents during their "exit interview."

"But anorexia and bulimia can be lifetime illnesses. We still haven't gotten to the root cause. Most times it has to do with the child's relationship to her parents –especially if she feels some pressure to be perfect in their eyes…sometimes it has to do with her feeling she has no control over her own life. But, you and Mrs. Roberts seem devoted to your daughter," the doctor continued. "Are you sure nothing traumatic has happened to her…maybe a neighbor who is a little too friendly, or a brother…"

"Our neighbors are all decent people!" her father had snapped. "She has no brothers, and if you are implying that I…"

"Now, now, Mr. Roberts, I'm implying no such thing," the doctor interrupted. Turning to Claire who had retreated to a chair in the corner of the office, he said, "Well, young lady, are you ready to go home?"

"Yes, sir," she answered in a flat tone.

"You will be a good girl and keep eating, won't you?" He spoke to Claire as if she were a child of seven, not sixteen.

"Yes, sir."

"Good. I'll see you next week when you come for your weight check and therapy session." He ushered the family to the door, shaking Cal's hand, patting his wife's shoulder reassuringly.

"Remember, Claire, you have to eat if you want to live."

Claire exited the office deliberately keeping her gaze ahead, not looking at the doctor. At his words, she smiled faintly, then followed her parents outside into the bright, warm air.

"Now, remember, Claire, we've told everyone that you have been visiting your sister, helping out with the children," her father instructed on the ride home. "We don't want anyone to find out where you've been. Do you understand, Claire?"

"Yes, sir," Claire answered in the same flat tone. She stared out the window, looking back at the low brick buildings of the hospital. She could see several patients walking with a nurse beneath the oak trees that grew in the front yard.

"You'll have exams to make up. I stopped by the school yesterday to talk with your guidance counselor," her father continued. "Good thing you pulled this stunt close to the end of the year or you'd have to repeat the whole semester."

Claire made no response as they pulled up in front of their house. She was startled by the greenness of the grass and the fullness of the leaves in the maple trees out front.

"You're not going to shame us, again, Claire," her father said as they drove up the driveway. "Your mother has strict instructions what to feed you and you are going to eat every bite. Do you hear me?" Cal raised his voice. Claire let her mind wander around the yard, pausing at each bloom, each new sign of summer.

As they walked up the front sidewalk, her father said, "I don't understand you, Claire. Your mother and I have given you everything and this is how you repay us."

"Will you just let her alone?" Mary spoke for the first time since they left the hospital. "She wouldn't be sick if you didn't put so much pressure on her to stay thin…to not become a "fat cow" like Mrs. Neal, like me. Just let her alone!"

Claire had never heard her mother express this much anger openly, outside her parent's bedroom. Her father stopped halfway up the front steps, his clinched fists and shallow breaths revealing his deep agitation.

"Don't you ever speak to me that way in front of our daughter. It is not my fault she's a loony. You have spoiled her all her life. It's made her weak –just like you."

Claire covered her ears with her hands and ran inside, unable to lock her bedroom door. She pulled the comforter from the duffel bag, flinging underwear and socks onto the floor. Wrapping herself inside, grateful for the warmth despite the ninety-degree heat, she closed her eyes and began to sing "Moon River" to drown out the angry words shooting up the stairwell. It was the only one of her mother's morning songs that she could remember.

As the argument became more heated, she sang louder and louder, so that, by the time she reached the final stanza, her voice was no longer recognizable. The last word was drawn out into a wail. "Meeee!"

Her parents stopped arguing, startled by the inhuman sound coming from their daughter's room.

"Meeee," Claire screamed until her voice failed and the word became a sob. She buried her face in her pillow, let the tears soak the front of the pillowcase. Hearing her parents running noisily up the stairs, Claire quickly closed her eyes and pretended to be asleep. She held her breath as they burst into her room, could feel the heat of their out-of- shape bodies as they leaned over her bed, their voices now lowered to urgent whispers between gasps for air. As her parents tiptoed to the door and closed it behind them with a soft click, Claire released her own pent-up breath. Then she let go of the tension in her muscles until her arms and legs seemed to float on the surface of some dark mysterious river flowing from an unseen source and into a painless night.

"Me," Claire spoke out loud to the muffin crumbs on the table.

"What was that?" Nita asked, touching her sister's arm, bringing her back to the present, motioning towards the scattered bits of muffin, nuts, and dried apples spread out messily on the table.

"You have to eat," Nita encouraged.

Claire sat up suddenly and looked directly at her sister, "If you want to live," she finished Nita's sentence, then repeated the end slowly, pausing slightly between each word.

"If…you…want…to…live." She grabbed the corners of the napkin, drawing them up into a moist ball containing the remnants of her muffin, then rose slowly, took two steps, and dropped it into the trash receptacle that stood beside the outside door.

Chapter VI

"I'm worried about you, Claire." Nita placed one hand on her sister's outstretched arm. They had walked to Dulaney's Market in silence from the coffee shop. Claire was in the process of filling a plastic shopping basket with cans of Max' favorite food. The basket was already too heavy for Claire to hold with one hand and she placed it on the floor, stacking the cans inside.

"Leave room for some human food," Nita chided her sister, trying to wrest a smile from her somber face.

Claire seemed not to hear. Satisfied she could fit no more cans in the basket, she leaned over, grabbed the handles with both hands and tried to lift it off the floor. Nita could see the stringy muscles in her arm quiver with the effort.

"O.K., little Sis, I'll make a deal with you," Nita struggled to keep her voice light. "You put five cans back, fill the space with milk, bread, and some fruit, and I'll carry it to the checkout counter. What good are all those cans for Max if his owner is too weak to open them?"

Claire released the handles and stood up, groaning at the stiffness in her back. She felt weak, the adrenaline rush of anger at the coffee shop having dissipated on the walk to the store. She had no energy left to resist Nita's logic.

"O.K." Claire leaned over again, grabbing the top two cans and began placing them neatly on the shelf as Nita moved off to gather the food items Claire had agreed to.

"Just what do you think you're doing?" Claire had been too absorbed in her task to hear Mrs. Dulaney's footsteps behind her. "I said, what do you think you are doing?" Mrs. Dulaney repeated with an accusatory sharpness.

Claire visibly cringed at the question.

Suddenly, she was ten years old, her teacher leaning over her desk, then snatching a paper from beneath Claire's math test.

"Class," Mrs. Wainwright cooed, "it appears Claire has more important things to do than her school work. She thinks she's an artist. Well, we'll give her a one person show right up here on the bulletin board." Mrs. Wainwright had then walked to the side wall of the classroom and tacked the sheet to the cork board. The whole class could see that it contained the pictures of several hearts, pierced by arrows, with the initials "J.D." clearly printed inside. It hung there for several days during which time Claire was mercilessly teased. Even her friends had joined in the playground chant, "Claire loves Jeffrey, Claire loves Jeffrey."

The worst indignity of all was that the object of her affection, Jeffrey Downs, the smartest kid in the class and teased by the boys as a "wimp," had stopped talking to her. Comfortable in each other's presence, they had spent many recess periods sitting under the old oak tree beside the school fence. She was fascinated by his knowledge of Greek mythology and history, and he had been grateful for an audience.

Now, at recess, he joined the other boys' game of kickball, endured their taunts when he missed the ball or tripped on his way to the base. Claire was forced to watch the other girls jump rope and listen to their inane songs and ditties. They refused to let her have a turn, not that she would have wanted one, anyway. Even after Mrs. Wainwright took down her "artwork" and threw it away, Claire had spent the rest of the school year sitting alone on the playground.

"Are you deaf as well as dumb?" Mrs. Dulaney's harsh voice brought Claire back to the present.

"I was just...my sister said," Claire stammered.

"If you insist on taking more than you can pay for, at least bring it to the counter so someone who knows the proper way to arrange it on the shelf can put it back. This may not be Safeway, but we do have standards." Mrs. Dulaney grabbed the two cans Claire was holding and stood on her tiptoes to place them on the top shelf. She was a tiny woman with dull red hair, peppered with gray. She always wore a blue smock over her clothes, a white blouse, black slacks, and black shoes made of soft leather.

"Is your cat the only one who eats at your place?" The older woman fixed her eyes on the two collarbones that jutted out from the base of Claire's neck.

"Yes…I mean no." Claire's mind was filled with a mixture of a ten-year-old's guilt and adult humiliation. "My sister went to get some bread and milk…I do eat." Desperate not to evoke any more criticism from this fussy woman, she tried to laugh, as if it were a joke, but the sound was more like a rattle from deep in her throat.

Mrs. Dulaney reached up to place the last can on the shelf, slid it around and rotated it so that the front of the label was visible. "There," she said as she sank back on her heels and brushed her hands together, giving Claire a visual once-over that she did not attempt to hide.

"You know, you could do with a good home-cooked meal. I'll have Sean bring over a plate after I cook supper tonight." Mrs. Dulaney directed this last statement to herself, more than to Claire, nodding her head with satisfaction as she walked quickly back up the aisle to the cash register.

Claire was too stunned to move, or even protest. She tried to remember if she knew anyone named Sean, then recalled seeing a teenage boy sweeping the sidewalk in front of the store on Saturdays. He was wearing headphones and moving to the beat of the silent music. Claire had secretly laughed at his reddish hair, sticking out from the edges of an Orioles baseball cap that he wore backwards. She knew he must be related to the Dulaney's, but couldn't quite believe that anyone wearing baggy pants so low on his hips that the elastic band on his boxers showed, could possibly be "Mrs. Neat as a Pin's" son.

"You don't have to do that," she finally called to the shop owner's back, now out of hearing range. Claire leaned her head on the metal shelf for a moment, equally stunned by Mrs. Dulaney's kind gesture and the thought of some young kid showing up at her apartment door.

"Here we are." Nita materialized beside Claire, bending over with some difficulty to place a loaf of whole grain bread, half gallon of milk and some apples into the basket. She grabbed the handles and lifted the basket effortlessly off the floor, though Claire could hear her breath come in puffs as she moved up the aisle.

"Claire, come on," Nita called to her sister who was still leaning against the cat food shelf, lost in thought.

"Come on Claire," she called from the checkout counter, "we have to hurry or I'll be late for work at the hospital." Nita began placing the food and cans on the counter for Mrs. Dulaney to ring up. Claire could see her sister lean over as the older woman whispered something in her ear, nodding her head as if in agreement.

Claire tried to push down the anger that had boiled over at the coffee shop. She was sick and tired of people whispering about her, pitying her, giving her endless advice and their own formulas for happiness and health. This was her life, her mess, her pain, the world that she had created and must now live in, the world she deserved. Couldn't they accept that and just leave her alone?

All of these self-righteous thoughts propelled her down the aisle and out of the store. She passed the checkout counter without looking at her sister or Mrs. Dulaney, not even stopping when the older woman called, "I'll send Sean around this evening. You need to eat, you're too skinny. How do you expect to get a man looking like that?"

Nita paid the bill hurriedly and raced after Claire who was already halfway down the block. She was slowed by the excess weight of the groceries, shifting them to her hip the way she carried her babies.

"What's wrong with you?" she chided Claire once she had caught up. "Mrs. Dulaney was just being kind."

"No she wasn't, she was interfering in my life. I don't need her kindness. I don't need anyone's kindness. I just want to be left alone!" They had reached the marble stairs of Claire's apartment house. "I can take care of myself. I don't even need you." Claire looked down on her sister from the landing. She tried to imitate Nita's authoritative stance with legs apart and both fists resting on her protruding hipbones. Her eyes were wild and focused on her sister's open mouth.

Nita started to speak, her cheeks reddened by hurt and fury. But she couldn't seem to find the words to articulate the conflicting emotions she was feeling of anger, pity, love, and frustration. She looked up at

Claire, at the curls which stood out like corkscrews from her head. Her sister's neck was so thin that she could even see the blood pulsing to her brain. Nita could feel her own heart soften as she looked into Claire's dark-rimmed eyes that were flashing menacingly above the prominent cheek bones. Still, the pity she felt was not quite strong enough to overcome her indignation at being so summarily dismissed by someone whose clothes hung from her skinny limbs like a scarecrow's.

"Suit yourself." Nita placed the bag of groceries on the bottom step, propping it against the railing. "I'm late, anyway…certainly don't want to waste time where I am not needed."

Nita turned stiffly then walked away from the stairs and down the sidewalk, not once looking back. Claire watched her leave, surprised as she always was, with the grace of Nita's movement. Claire knew by the set of her sister's shoulders that she had pushed the last person who loved her away for good.

She made a mental note of everyone in her life who had left her, or rather everyone she had not had the strength to keep: her father, David, her child, and, now, Nita.

Her father had been the first to leave. Claire recalled the afternoon of her senior year of high school when she had come home to a silent house, too silent in retrospect. Her mother, usually engaged in housekeeping activities, failed to respond to Claire's call. She found Mary sitting in the living room, her back straight, hands folded in her lap, bloodshot eyes focused ahead.

"Mother, what's wrong?" Claire touched her shoulder, evoking no response. Alarmed, Claire started towards the phone on the lamp table beside the soft sofa where her father sat each evening to watch the news. The imprint of his body from the night before was still outlined in the cushions. Beside the phone she found a folded piece of paper bearing her mother's name. Claire recognized the handwriting. Suddenly lightheaded and queasy, her hand shaking the formal stationary her father used for business letters, Claire read its contents:

Dear Mary,

I can no longer live this lie. I stopped loving you years ago. You and the girls ask too much of me. I know I am not perfect, but your neediness has drained me dry. I am moving in with a woman who loves me and asks nothing in return. I will have my lawyer draw up a separation agreement. Tell Claire I intend to pay her college tuition and despite all the trouble and shame she has caused us, I still love her.

-Cal

Claire's knees gave way and she collapsed onto the sofa, burying her face into the headrest. She could smell her father's after-shave. It made her nauseous, yet she drew in deep breaths. "Trouble and shame," "trouble and shame," the words played over and over again in her mind like a stuck record.

Immersed in her own guilt and grief, Claire had forgotten about her mother until a soft sniff reminded her of the older woman's presence. She crawled across the carpet, burning her knees on the rough nap and grabbed onto her mother's legs. Mary did not move, made no attempt to comfort her daughter, too lost in her own deep misery.

"I did everything the doctors said. I ate everything on my plate. Daddy was proud of me. He told me he was. I don't understand…I did everything he said." The words spilled out sporadically between sobs. Claire clung to her mother's legs, wetting the nylon stockings with her tears until her energy was spent and the room became quiet again.

"It's not your fault," Claire barely recognized her mother's voice –it was flat and faint. "It's not your fault," she said reaching down to stroke her daughter's hair.

Mary rose, then, pushing Claire gently away. "I have to make supper."

Claire heard her mother clattering pans and dishes in the kitchen as she prepared the evening meal…as though nothing had happened…as though everything was still the same.

"Dinner's ready," her mother called sometime later. Claire, who was still kneeling beside the empty chair, did not feel like eating, could not believe her mother's passive behavior. She knew she caused her father to leave them. She knew she was the source of her parent's deep unhappiness. She knew she was the reason her father's place at the table was empty when she finally found the strength to walk to the kitchen.

Claire ached as she watched her mother stare through the steam rising from her dinner plate, hands clasped loosely in her lap. Claire was afraid to try and swallow, but did not want to cause her mother anymore pain. She forced bite after bite into her mouth, reminding herself to chew, though the food stuck in her dry throat.

Mary ate nothing, waited until Claire's plate was empty before wiping her own mouth with the clean napkin on which her hands had rested. Then, she picked up the two plates and dropped them in the sink.

"I think I'll go up and lie down for a while." Mary spoke to the open window above the sink, to the calico curtains that she had made herself, then turned and walked slowly upstairs. Claire heard her parents' door close softly, the creak of the bedsprings overhead, the silence that wafted down from the second floor until it filled the whole house. Claire listened a moment longer for some sign of life from her mother's room, but the silence only grew louder until Claire could stand it no more.

She attacked the dishes, scrubbing the pots and pans until she could see her face reflected in their bottoms. She washed down the counters and cabinets, scrubbed the floor on her hands and knees.

When there were no more surfaces in the kitchen to clean, she ran the vacuum in the living room, sucking invisible dust from the chairs and couch…sucking up any trace of his presence…his stench, his rot. Tears wet

Claire's face as she worked -at first, tears of sorrow and loss, but soon the hot tears of anger and hate. The roar from the vacuum drowned out the words, "trouble" and "shame," that still echoed in her head.

Finally spent from this physical frenzy, Claire collapsed onto the soft couch. Even though she was exhausted, her mind could not rest from its kaleidoscope of memories. Some were unpleasant: her father's angry voice through the wall at night; his cruelty towards her mother each morning; his face suffused with horror and loathing the night he undressed his daughter.

But, older memories of their life together when Claire was still a little girl, renewed the ache of her father's desertion. He had seemed different back then, more relaxed and less critical. They had been pals. She was his curly-haired princess whose presence could always evoke a proud smile even after his long days at work. On his days off, her father would sometimes take Claire for a walk in the park, sharing a foot-long hotdog beside the lake, even though they both knew it would spoil their appetite for dinner. Occasionally, they went on long drives in the country, stopping at their favorite fishing spot. Those afternoons seemed endless and wonderful to Claire. She could still hear her father's laughter at her attempt to perform a one-handed cartwheel and his concern when she fell. He was her very own Prince Charming, who loved only her and with whom she would live happily ever after.

Gradually, as Claire grew older, their relationship began to change. Her father seemed not even to notice her some days when he returned from work. Still a child, Claire interpreted his behavior as rejection of her and as he became more distracted and distant, she was convinced she had done something wrong and that she no longer deserved his love.

It was only as an adult that Claire learned of the near failure of her father's business, his own struggle with depression that exacerbated the already growing rift between her parents. But, how was she, as a child, to know his behavior towards his family was merely his way of coping with his own feelings of failure? How was she to know that his constant criticism of his youngest daughter and his wife was a feeble attempt to control at least part of his life, since, outside their home, he had control over nothing?

Unable to stop the flood of regrets and memories, Claire climbed the stairs to her room, tiptoeing so as not to wake her mother. Exhausted, she crawled into her bed, wrapping her body inside the butterfly quilt, and drifted back to a time when she had felt unconditionally loved.

When she awoke to the morning light, her mind was clear and fresh for a moment -that is, until she remembered that she had driven her father away.

The pain of that realization was quickly pushed away by the smell of bacon snaking up the stairs and into Claire's nostrils. She could hear the familiar sizzle and pop as she rubbed the sand from her eyes and stretched her cramped arms and legs. She could hear something else, something strong and rhythmic...her mother's voice.

The music continued as Claire walked downstairs and entered the kitchen, just as Mary was placing two plates with scrambled eggs and toast on the table. The older woman greeted her daughter with a radiant smile, then finished her song with a triumphant finale that bounced off the walls, chasing away the quiet of the night before.

"We don't need him, Claire," Mary said between bites after they both were seated. Claire glanced at her father's empty place, spotlighted by the morning sun that streamed through the window, then back to her mother's face. She realized she had never seen her mother look happier.

"We will survive," Mary stopped chewing. "Look at me, Claire." She forced her daughter to look into her clear eyes. "We will survive."

"I know," Claire replied, reaching up to smooth her tangled hair. "I know."

Chapter VII

A car horn startled Claire back to the present and she sat down heavily on the top step. Out of the corner of her eye, she saw Nita round the corner at the end of the block, and Claire reflexively rubbed the emptiness in her chest, bringing her gaze back to the grocery bag six steps below.

"I will survive, just like Mom and I did," she muttered. "I don't need anyone." She pushed herself up to standing, feeling lightheaded, and gripped the railing, sliding her hand along for support as she walked down the stairs. Still holding the rail, she reached over and grabbed the paper handles and attempted to straighten her knees, using the stronger muscles in her legs to lift the heavy contents.

To her surprise, she managed to lift the bag two inches off of the step, dangling it from one arm as she used the rail to climb back to the landing, bringing each foot up to meet the other like a toddler's first attempt at climbing stairs.

One step away from the landing, she began to silently congratulate herself, when the handles pulled away from the bag with a sickening rip. Her hand shot up as the load lightened and she looked down just as the bag split, spilling its contents onto the stairwell. Time slowed as the loaf of bread tumbled down towards the sidewalk. The plastic container of milk split open on the step's marble edge. Some of the white liquid shot out in all directions, the rest pouring down the stairs like a foamy water-fall. Apples bounced like rubber balls, rolling away at the base of the steps. But, worst of all, the small round discs of cat food clattered down to the sidewalk, then dispersed in all directions –into the street, the gutter, and under parked cars. She watched helplessly as one can rolled slowly to the curb, hung precariously over the edge, then tipped over into the abyss.

Claire began to laugh. "I deserve this," she repeated as she melted down into a heap on the top step, surveying the carnage below. "I deserve this," she chanted. "I deserve this," her voice rose and filled the city block. A woman walking on the other side of the street pulled up her collar and hurried past. A jogger turned around and ran the other way. An elderly lady poked her head from behind a window blind, staring at the scattered food and the thin woman as her final cry died out into hysterical laughter.

Just as at the diner with Mark, Claire's body convulsed with giggles she could not control. Everything was so funny. She could not have made a bigger mess if she had tried. The loaf of bread protruded from a split in its plastic covering, exposing several slices to the noonday sun. The empty milk carton still dripped remnants of its former contents. An apple that had been flattened to twice its diameter by a passing car, lay in the middle of the street like road kill. The cat food cans scattered as far away as the eye could see, were being batted around by a truck's tires like hockey pucks on the ice.

Claire laughed uncontrollably at the ridiculous scene, until her face was wet with tears. They were not happy tears, but those of a defeated young woman whose sorrow was now exposed to the sun-warmed air, like the stale slices of bread.

She buried her head in her arms, resting her forehead on her drawn-up knees, closing her eyes to the scene. Silently, she prayed for the peace of oblivion -for sleep, for unconsciousness, for death –anything to blot out the mess she had made of her life.

Soon, the images behind her eyelids disappeared into a blessed blackness. The words she was still repeating became softer, fainter, until they, too, were gone…and all that remained was a low buzz, a hum in her ear that she recognized as the inexplicable flow of blood through her veins. She concentrated on that sound which pulsed louder with each beat of her heart. Claire willed it all to stop –the hum, the pulse, her heart, her life…but the hypnotic beat continued.

The muscles in her shoulders began to relax. Her body felt fluid as if it contained no bones, like Max when he did not want to be picked up. She felt herself begin to slide down the step. But something impeded the slow meltdown of her body onto the sidewalk below

-something solid and steady and warm -a pressure on both of her knees.

Slightly irritated, but not alarmed, Claire reached out with one hand to brush this obstacle away, then pulled it back, repelled by the feel of rough wool. Without lifting her head, she opened her eyes. Several cans of cat food were stacked beside her feet. The loaf of bread, tucked inside its plastic wrapper, was wedged against the railing on the step below. Beside the bread, and directly in front of where she was sitting, were a man's scuffed shoes, partly hidden by the frayed cuffs of a pair of gray slacks.

With horror, Claire felt the pressure of a hand on her shoulder and could hear someone's slow even breathing. Someone was bending over her, and she realized she had to act quickly. Grabbing the railing with one hand, she used the other to lash out against her attacker, and stood up. The man, caught off guard, lost his balance, fell backwards, flapping his arms ineffectually, and landed on his back with a dull thump at the base of the stairs.

Claire looked down at his still form. His coat was splayed open on either side exposing a dirty shirttail that seemed to escape from the bottom of two sweater vests. A plaid scarf was knotted at the man's reddened neck.

For a moment, she didn't know whether to run or call for help. Holding tightly to the rail, she inched down the steps, keeping her eyes warily on the body, tensed to defend herself should he suddenly spring up. No sound emitted from between his slack lips. She could see no movement in his outstretched arms and legs, not even the rise and fall of the stranger's chest.

"I've killed him," she panicked, about to flee, when a groan drew her focus to the man's face. Cautiously she bent over his inert body, looked into his opened eyes for a sign of life, was startled when the pupils, wide and dilated, surrounded by deep blue, shifted to meet her gaze.

"The Duke of Danvers Street at your service, m'lady," the man croaked just before his eyes rolled back and his head fell limply to the side. Claire's mind raced backwards to the day before, to another time she had seen those eyes. She remembered the man's words, how he had called her pretty, had sent her home when she was lost.

Claire stood for a moment looking down at his dirty, unshaven face. Afraid to touch him with her hand, she nudged his lifeless arm with her toe, just as she had a stray dog that had run out in front of her car several years before. The man did not move nor make any sound.

"I've killed him," she said again. Suddenly aware something needed to be done, she searched the sidewalk and street for someone who might come to their rescue. The block was empty, except for the parked cars that lined the street.

"I've got to get help." She turned and tried to run up the stairs, tripping once and knocking her shin against an edge. "I've got to get help." She pushed open the heavy door, groped her way down the dark hall to her apartment door, and tried to turn the handle. Too late she remembered the key was inside, that she had left earlier without taking her purse. She leaned her head against the door, trying to clear her brain with deep even breaths.

"I'll get the landlord." A plan materialized through the panicky fog. "He has a phone...he can help," she muttered, making her way back to the light from the front windows. The landlord's apartment was on the third floor. When she reached the bottom of the stairwell, she looked up at the open space through which she could see the top story ceiling.

"Mr. Grimes," she called weakly. "I need help." Her voice echoed off the dirty walls. She strained to hear some response, then called again. "Mr. Grimes, please come...I need help." Again, there was silence. Claire slumped over the newel post, knew she would not be able to climb the three flights to his door. Rallying her last bit of strength, she called again, "Mr. Grimes, I've killed someone!"

Just then, Claire heard the rattling of a lock. She turned as the door to the front downstairs apartment opened a crack. She could barely see her elderly neighbor's wrinkled face looking out suspiciously, the security chain still attached to her door.

"What's all this racket?" her neighbor whispered. "Who's there? Go away or I'll call the police." The woman's voice quavered as if from fear.

"It's me, Mrs. Burton, Claire...your neighbor. I need help. I've killed someone." Claire's voice was high, revealing her growing panic.

"Claire? Claire who? I don't know any Claire. Go away!" Mrs. Burton slammed the door shut. Claire could hear the deadbolt click and the woman's quick footsteps as she moved away. She staggered to the door, banging on it with her fists.

"Mrs. Burton, please, I live next door...remember?" She waited a moment, hearing only the blood rushing in her ears. "I think I've killed someone. Please let me in so I can call 911!"

"Go away!"

Claire turned and leaned against the locked door. Tears of frustration and anguish poured down her face like the spilt milk. She felt herself slipping down onto the floor. The hallway became darker until she could not even see the spot of light on the worn rug beside her feet, until she could hear nothing, not even the pulsing of blood in her ears, not even her neighbor's continued shouts for her to go away -nothing...

Chapter VIII

"Mark, I need to talk to you. I think I'm hallucinating. Please call as soon as you get this message," Claire told her therapist's voice mail. She had called his office a half an hour after her landlord had found her sleeping in the hallway. Assuming she was drunk, he had pulled her to her feet, dragged her down the hallway, and shoved her into her apartment, opening the door with his master key. Her incessant babbling about having killed someone on the front steps only confirmed his theory of her inebriation. Having just come back home from the laundry mat, he knew he would have noticed a dead body on the sidewalk, although, he had been puzzled by the neatly stacked food on the front steps.

"Now, sleep it off. I can't have any drunks living in my building. You'd better clean up your act or you are out of here, missy," Mr. Grimes warned. He was surprisingly strong, given his small stature and wiry frame, and had slammed the door loudly behind him as he left. Claire could hear his determined tread. She sat on the bed, too stunned to move, concentrating on each footfall on the stairs until the clang of his door echoed down to the first floor.

Glancing around the apartment, Claire found Max perched in his favorite spot on the windowsill. She rubbed her aching arms and neck, trying to clear the muddle in her brain. She dared not close her eyes, knowing the image of the stranger's lifeless body would still be there in her visual memory. With horror, she began to remember the dream she had while "sleeping" in the hall: the stranger's splayed-out form had begun to grow fur. His hands had become paws, his dull lifeless pupils had become slits surrounded by yellow, not round ones, rimmed in blue.

Max' soft meow was a welcome distraction. She knew Max was hungry, that Mr. Grimes had mentioned the food still stacked on the steps, but could not summon the courage to go out and retrieve the cans. He had not seen the body, however, and Claire began to wonder if it had all been a dream, if her mind had finally slipped over the edge of depression into psychosis.

Max meowed again, jumping down silently as only cats can do, and walked to his empty food dish. He stood looking down for a moment then up at Claire with the same disgust he had exhibited towards the plate's previous contents.

"O.K., O.K.," Claire gave in. "I'll go get your food." She rose stiffly from the bed, opened the door, careful to set the latch so she could get back in without her key.

The distance between her apartment and the front door might as well have been a mile, such effort did it take for Claire to place one heavy foot in front of the other. With each step, her stomach tightened, her heart raced faster. What if he was still lying there? What would she do? What if he wasn't there, had never been there at all? What if she had imagined the whole incident? What if she had finally gone completely mad?

By the time she reached the heavy door, she did not know which scenario would be worse. She leaned her head briefly against the edge of the doorframe, took a deep breath and opened the door, just far enough to stick her head out and view the scene of her latest debacle.

The afternoon sun had dipped low on the horizon and its rays slanted directly into her eyes. She closed them quickly against the glare, counted to ten, then shielding them with one hand, opened the lids cautiously. Looking down, she saw the landing was empty except for the frayed "Welcome" mat directly in front of the door. She let her eyes descend the staircase one step at a time. On the third step from the top stood the two stacks of cat food. Apples, she was sure she had not noticed before, were balanced on top of each stack like balls in a circus act. The loaf of bread was still where she had seen it, securely pushed up against the side rail. At least she had not imagined those, Claire thought with relief. But, she wondered how they had regrouped themselves from their disparate sites after the bag broke, if the stranger had not been real.

Cautiously, Claire looked down to the sidewalk at the base of the steps, the concrete reflecting back the bright sun. Save for the familiar cracks and a discarded hamburger wrapper, it was bare -no man, no spread out coat, no creased brown shoes, no blood -swept clean like a crime scene where all the fingerprints had been carefully wiped away.

Claire walked out onto the landing and sat on the top step. With this corroboration of Mr. Grimes' story and its implications for Claire's sanity, she thought of the last time she had sat there, only an hour before... before she had gone over the edge like that can of cat food, into the world of total madness.

"He was here," the small remaining part of her rational mind argued. "I know he was here. But, I killed him. Dead people just don't get up and walk away. I know I would have heard the sirens if someone had called an ambulance...even in the hall." She was frantically clinging to this logic. "I know I wasn't that out of it. And, besides, they would have searched the building for his killer. The front door is not locked...they would have come in and found her -me—the murderer...and I would have confessed."

Another part of her brain argued back: "What if he hadn't really been here at all? What if I only imagined him? What if some passing good Samaritan placed the food on the steps?"

By now, Claire's mutterings had drawn attention from passersby. She did not notice them. She was lost, again, in the past.

Claire was thinking about her childhood boyfriend, Jeffrey Downs, who had suffered what the doctors called a "schizophrenic break" his first year of college.

According to the story Claire had heard, he had locked himself in the science lab of the Ivy League college where he had gone on full scholarship, threatening to mix two combustible chemicals. Apparently, voices had told him that the dean was the anti-Christ and it was his holy mission to destroy this fiend along with the campus that harbored him.

There had been no warning, Claire remembered. Jeffrey sailed through high school academically and had become quite popular after growing into a 6-foot, 2-inch body and developing muscles. Despite his position as a guard on the basketball team, he had kept his grades up, graduating as valedictorian. His address to the student body had been short and powerful, exhorting his fellow seniors to overcome obstacles to their success and go out to conquer the world.

Claire had lost track of Jeffrey after high school, knew only that he had gone away to college. She was shocked to learn that he had dropped out of school and had been institutionalized for six months, during which time, he was heavily sedated to protect the other patients. He had then gone home to live with his parents, rarely setting foot outside their house.

"Such a waste," Claire lamented, drifting back to their sessions beneath the shade of the old oak, listening to Jeffrey recount with great feeling and detail the adventures of the Greek gods.

What saddened Claire the most when she heard of J.D.'s illness, was the contrast between her life, then, and his. She had been well on the road to recovery before her father left, having woken the morning after her disastrous return home from the hospital, resolved to save her parents' marriage. Seeing herself as the source of their discord, she followed the doctor's orders, returning to the hospital for weekly weight checks and group therapy sessions.

Gradually, the impact of each new pound lessened until, having reached a "normal" healthy weight, and what her therapist felt was an equilibrium in her emotional status, Claire was pronounced "cured" and released from care. Her parents' relationship appeared to heal as well and she rejoiced when each night passed without the drone of an argument through the plaster wall.

Consequently, her father's abrupt departure was a shock, but, instead of sending her into an emotional tailspin, it gave her room to breathe. Her mother seemed brighter, more articulate during their meals together. Most of the conversations centered on Claire's activities at school and her growing list of friends, both male and female.

Claire's father had been generous in the divorce settlement, preempting his wife's need to claim his leaving as "abandonment." In addition to child support, he agreed to pay all four years' tuition for Claire to attend a nearby state college where she enrolled the fall after her high school graduation.

At first, she came home every weekend to do her laundry and look in on her mother. But, Mary, at the urging of her daughters, had started dating a lawyer from the firm that had hired her to do secretarial work and was out most weekend nights.

Claire was amazed by the transformation of her shy, sometimes dowdy, mother into a witty, well-dressed businesswoman. Mary's new life left her youngest daughter free to enjoy her life as a college co-ed. Claire dated several boys, accompanying them to the school pub and an occasional fraternity party. But, their need to get drunk, even on weeknights, bored her and she immersed herself, instead, in her Special Education major.

During her free time and for extra credit, Claire volunteered at a local elementary school. It was there that she had met David. Claire rarely allowed herself to dwell on those first happy years with the love of her life, wondering if David would have still chosen to marry her if he had known the misery that lay ahead for them both.

Just then, a garbage truck, groaning under the weight of refuse, pulled up noisily to the curb. Forced to abandon her reverie and hoping to avoid any interaction with the garbage men, who were now walking towards the bins at the base of the steps, Claire quickly loaded her arms with the cat food and apples, dangling the loaf of bread from two fingers. Somehow, she was able to turn the handle and open the wooden door, walking carefully down the hall so as not to drop the purchases again.

Max jumped down and ran to her as soon as she entered the room, circling and rubbing against her legs, meowing piteously. Claire nearly fell on the way to the kitchen counter where she deposited the food, grabbing a runaway apple before it could splat on the floor.

"Here you go, Maxie. Mommy's got some good food for her baby," Claire crooned as she pulled the can opener from a drawer and struggled to open the can, straining with each turn of the handle. Max' cries became louder, more piercing.

"Shh, Max, we don't want to bother Mrs. Burton." Claire sped up her efforts, gagging slightly as the fish odor poured from the open can. With a fork, she flaked the food out onto Max' empty dish. He pushed his nose against her hand, greedily grabbing big bites before she even could empty the tin. She could hear him swallow without chewing and knew she would be cleaning up undigested kitty food in a minute.

"Slow down, Max," she cautioned. "You're going to throw up." But Max paid no attention to his owner. She knelt down beside him, stroking the fur on his back and sleek sides. After licking the bowl clean, he then ran his tongue over his lips fastidiously and walked leisurely back to the window. Before hopping back up to the sill, he stretched out his front paws and leaned back on his haunches. Then, once on his perch, he settled down into a contented ball of fur.

Distracted momentarily by these feline antics and pleased she had finally fulfilled her duties as a responsible pet owner, Claire rinsed the fork and threw the empty can in the garbage. With disgust, she noted that its odor had strengthened from that morning, when Nita was searching for coffee. She resolved to take the bin out back that afternoon.

Weak from hunger and her ordeal, Claire collapsed onto the bed, leaning back onto the soft cushions. As soon as she closed her eyes, the stranger's limp body appeared, sending a sudden electric jolt of panic through her arms and legs. She sat up suddenly, debating his reality again.

"Maybe I'm just hungry," she reasoned. "I've heard hunger can cause hallucinations." Determined that was the answer to the bizarre events of the morning, she rose and crossed to the small kitchen. Opening the refrigerator door, she was startled anew by its Spartan contents. Grabbing the half-empty carton of yogurt, the rinsed fork from the drain, and an apple from the counter, she returned to the table, sinking down into the single chair. The lid on the yogurt container seemed stuck, until it flew off into the air landing face down on the carpet. Claire decided to pick it up later.

The first bite of yogurt, with its sweet-tartness, caused the muscles inside her mouth to contract. She moved the creamy glob around with her tongue before swallowing it with some difficulty. The second bite was not as shocking and she could feel its coolness slide down her throat and into her hollow stomach. When she could see the bottom of the container, she picked up the apple and took a bite. Juice squirted from the corners of her mouth, but the apple skin was so tough, that she spit its remains out into the yogurt container, after having chewed for what seemed an eternity.

Claire felt full and heavy after this repast, dull witted, as if her body could only perform one function at a time, digestion now beating out her attempts to think.

Nonetheless, she forced herself to review the events of the day, starting with her sister's visit, her angry gesture at the coffee shop, Mrs. Dulaney's well-meaning but bizarre offer of dinner. She grimaced as she recalled looking down on Nita from the top steps, effectively telling her to "go to hell," then the empty ache in her chest as her sister complied. She remembered the weight of the grocery bag, the slow motion dispersal of its contents after the handle broke. She remembered sitting on the steps and sinking down into her normal pattern of mental escape from unpleasantness. But then she gasped, for she could still feel the pressure of the man's hands on her knees, his warm breath on the back of her head, could still see his bright blue eyes and hear the kindness of his voice before he died.

"He was real," Claire spoke out loud. Max gazed at her sleepily.

"I know he was real. I am not crazy. I killed him… that is a fact." Claire banged her fist on the table to emphasize the last words, repeating them again as she picked up the phone on the small table beside her bed and dialed Mark's number. At that moment, another voice, unspoken, asked, "But where did he go?"

"I am not crazy," she muttered into the ringing receiver, "or am I?" just as the computerized voice said with its maddening monotone, "If you wish to leave a message…"

Chapter IX

"But, he was there...I could feel his breath," Claire argued with Mark the next morning. Despite his busy schedule, Mark had agreed to meet with her between 11:30 and 12:30, his normal lunch hour. She balked at his suggestion that they hold their session at the diner. Claire did not want to return to the site of her public meltdown —did not want to face the kind waitress, not knowing if she had the strength to avoid a repeat of the emotional scene that had marred their first encounter.

Besides, she had already risked being recognized at the diner the evening before. As soon as she had left the voice message for Mark, Claire walked the ten blocks from her apartment to the diner, fueled by the yogurt and her desperation to find out who the man was that she had killed -or, what had really happened to him.

It was dusk by the time she reached her destination. Only a dim light shone through the diner's plate glass windows —a "closed" sign hanging on the door. She was relieved to find the restaurant only served breakfast and lunch.

So anxious was she to reach Danvers Street before dark, Claire had tried to run the entire way, crossing streets without stopping or waiting for the "Walk" light to flash. The fatigue and lethargy that she had felt for weeks was dissipated by the presence of so much adrenaline. Occasionally a sharp pain in her side brought her to an abrupt stop and she would have to bend over to gulp a mouthful of air. Once, she paused in the middle of an intersection, but Claire did not notice the squeal of tires or curses flung her direction from the angry drivers. She was on a mission, a righteous mission, to prove her sanity even if it meant confronting the fact that she had taken someone's life.

Claire had no clear plan when she set out –only an overwhelming need to return to the place that she had first encountered this man. If nothing else, she planned to stop every cab on that block, hoping "Joe" could tell her something about the blue-eyed angel, or, at least, reassure her of his existence.

Spent from the exertion of her manic run, Claire leaned heavily against the brick wall beside the diner, taking great gulps of air, massaging the pain in her side. All the while, she kept her eyes open, scanning the street, searching each car, each pedestrian that passed.

Several times, she heard footsteps from the direction she was not looking. Turning expectantly, she would find herself facing a businessman hurrying home or a young punk who returned her look with an intimidating stare of his own.

As the glow from the setting sun faded behind the two and three-story buildings that lined the street, home to pawn shops, cigarette and liquor stores, and the diner, Claire's determination was gradually replaced by fear. It was a strange mixture of fear for her own safety, superceded by the growing possibility that the object of her search was no more real than the illusion that Mark could ever care for her as woman, not just a client.

Claire willed herself to stand sentry, despite the ache in her legs and back, the dimming of the daylight, the decrease in pedestrian traffic. A soft wind picked the curls up off of her forehead. She turned to face it head on, hoping the cool slap of air would keep her alert. She closed her eyes as the breeze blew the hair back from her face, let it enter her nostrils and mouth, chilling the superheated membranes inside, as if it could cleanse her of her guilt.

She did not notice the cab that pulled up and stopped at the curb in front of her, until its driver honked the horn for the second time. She strained to see inside, but the light from the overhead streetlight, which had just come on, cast a dark shadow on the cab's interior. Claire recognized it as being from the same company as the one that had taken her home. "Was it only yesterday?" she asked herself.

Hesitating a moment to gather courage, Claire walked over to the passenger side and bent down to look at the driver, just as the window lowered.

"Heh, ain't you the lady from the diner? Do you need a ride?"

Claire drew back a step, placing a little distance between herself and the unseen speaker.

"Remember me? Joe?" This time he leaned over towards Claire's side of the vehicle far enough for the streetlight to catch his features.

At once, Claire recognized the deep lines slanting slightly upwards from the driver's eyes, "laugh lines" she had seen framed in the cab's rearview mirror.

"What are you doing here this late? This ain't a good neighborhood for a pretty lady to be alone in at night," Joe cautioned.

"I had hoped to see the man who helped me, who paid the cab fare." Claire looked at Joe expectantly, discouraged by his puzzled countenance.

"You know, the man you called "the Duke" or some kind of royal title like that." Claire was so anxious to hear his response, she opened the passenger door and slid in sideways on the front seat, one foot still touching the pavement, a move that would have shocked her in its carelessness a few days before.

"Oh, yeah —the Duke of Danvers Street, himself," Joe's eyes narrowed, the laugh lines nearly touching as he smiled.

"Yes, that's him," Claire slurred her words, thrilled at the confirmation of the man's existence. "Have you seen him recently, I mean, has he been around this afternoon?" Claire could not contain the verbal avalanche. "I want to thank him for helping me. He was so kind."

"Slow down, lady," Joe kidded, "There ain't no fire." Joe realized his mirth was not mirrored in Claire's eyes that had grown large and moist.

"Oh, the Duke comes and goes. Some days, you can find him here walking from one end of the block to the other -helping old ladies across the street, carrying groceries for some young mother, doling out money to me to drive some poor sucker home…Oh, no offense intended, lady."

Claire did not really mind being lumped into the category of "poor suckers," but she wished the cabby would answer her questions.

"But have you seen him this afternoon? Has he been here today?" she pleaded.

"Haven't seen him since I drove you home. Like I said, he's mysterious…shows up, does his good deeds, and disappears. I don't even know his real name. Me and the boys gave him the name of "the Duke" on account of the way he walks -slow-like, with his head held high like he was somebody." Joe's attention was drawn to an elderly lady standing across the street, waving her arm at him.

"There's Mrs. Sorrentino. It's Bingo night at the Catholic center. Sorry, got to go. My advice to you, lady, is to get yourself home before it's completely dark. Good luck finding the 'Duke'."

Claire took her cue, slid out of the seat and closed the car door. Just before Joe started off, she spoke through the still open window. "My name is Claire McKinney. My number is in the phonebook. If you see him, please tell him to call me. I want to thank him…" The last sentence was directed at the back of Joe's head as he pulled away, acknowledging her request with a wave. The sight of his pointed hairline above the same light blue shirt that he had worn when he had driven her home, left her feeling lonely.

Claire stood watching as Joe picked up his fare and drove off. She felt the cool breeze on her cheek, but it was colder now and it made her shiver. Her clothes, still damp from her walk, began to feel uncomfortable in the night air.

Reluctantly, she started the long trek home, hugging her arms around her to contain her body heat. Under other circumstances, she would have been afraid as she walked the mostly empty city blocks, passing alleys filled with overflowing garbage bins, recessed entryways where a mugger could lurk unseen.

Claire's mind was focused elsewhere than her immediate environs. On one hand, she mused, the mission had been successful. She had found Joe, someone who confirmed that the stranger existed, had helped her, and was not just a figment of a psychotic mind. On the other, Joe had not seen him since the preceding afternoon. He could be anywhere –home with his family (which she doubted), sleeping in a shelter, or stretched out on a slab in the city morgue.

The closer Claire got to her apartment building, the more certain she was of the last scenario. It made sense. He had shown up to help her again. She had knocked him off the steps. He had hit his head and died. Someone had scraped him off the sidewalk and hauled him away while she "slept" in the hallway.

As she reached the stairs of her building, Claire stopped, staring at the cement, at its familiar cracks. It all looked so innocent, so benign, in the soft glow of the street light, not like a murder weapon at all. But, then, it had been her own hand that had pushed him. That was the real weapon. She closed her eyes, rubbing her palms together in an attempt to wipe them clean.

"But someone would have come looking for me," the rational part of her brain argued. "I would have heard the ambulance. Maybe, he wasn't real after all. Maybe, I just imagined the whole thing. What is happening to me?" She spoke the last sentence out loud to the night sky. Mrs. Burton pulled back her blind a crack, then shut it quickly. Mr. Grimes, who kept his front window always open, leaned out to shoo away whatever riff-raff had chosen his stoop for a meeting place. But the steps were empty, luminescent in the combined light from the lamp and the rising moon.

Claire was already inside, hoping Mark had left a message. The thought, "I need help," propelling her down the hall. So anxious was she to check her messages, she didn't even stop to examine the brown paper bag that she tripped over in front of her apartment door. Not even the tantalizing smells of tomato sauce, fresh oregano, and basil that seeped out of the bag could slow her down. All she cared about was finding her key, opening the door, and pushing the "play" button of her answering machine, whose flashing light was reflected in Max' glowing eyes.

Chapter X

"Claire," Mark raised his voice to get her attention. Claire jerked her hand up to touch her hair, then reached back to tighten the rubber band that was holding her ponytail, frustrated by the stubborn strands that still tickled her cheek.

"Sorry." She felt chastised by his impatient tone. "Maybe he's starting to get sick of me…just like Nita," she thought. "Maybe he, too, will walk out of my life."

"My mind was wandering," she spoke out loud.

"Seems like it's been doing that a lot lately, Claire. What happens? Where do you go?" Mark's tone was gentle again.

"I don't know, exactly." Claire struggled to describe the wet darkness into which she escaped when the reality of her life became unbearable. "It feels safe…as if I'm wrapped in a quilt…everything blotted out by warmth and darkness."

"You feel safe there, Claire," Mark encouraged.

"Yes."

"Safe from what?" Mark did not want to lose this line of thought.

"From everything, I guess." Claire touched her hair again, found a loose strand and curled it around her finger. She wasn't sure she wanted to talk to Mark anymore about her "lapses" of consciousness —afraid if she did, she would lose the ability to find her way back to the comforting numbness.

"Can you go there now, Claire?"

This was such a strange request, Claire did not immediately answer. Actually, she did not know the answer. His question seemed a threat to this private world —her world —a place she had fled to years ago to escape her father's constant criticism, her mother's weakness, all the doctors and teachers who tried to control her life, the death of the baby and her marriage. It was her secret corner, hers alone.

Mark sat patiently waiting for her response. He could see by the expression on her face that some internal dialogue was taking place. He did not want to push her, knew this process of self-disclosure was brittle, would break into pieces if forced to unfold too quickly.

He also knew that his words had the power to push her to that place for good, so he gently said, "Claire, it's up to you. It would help me to know what it's like for you when you go there. I know it feels good to be there, but I think it's getting in the way of your recovery. It's keeping you from facing the problems that brought you here in the first place. Do you want to be well, Claire?" Mark leaned forward in his chair, looking directly into her eyes.

Claire glanced away, irritated by his inability to take seriously what had happened to her, what she had done to the Duke, the reason she wanted to talk to him in the first place.

"Mark, I've killed someone. Don't you understand? I've killed someone, or, rather, I think I have…or, maybe, I imagined the whole thing…maybe I'm crazy." Claire buried her face in her sweaty hands then drew them away and looked up at her therapist with bloodshot and unfocused eyes. "I don't know anymore, it's just… He was so kind…"

"Claire, do you want to be well?" His frank stare weakened her resolve to keep the conversation centered on the events of the day before.

"I don't know," she answered.

"Let me see if I can help you go to your safe place, then. Maybe things will seem clearer. Close your eyes." Mark's voice was soft, rhythmic.

Still feeling uneasy, Claire decided to comply.

"Listen to my voice, Claire. Think only of my words. They are your only thought, Claire. Your mind is a blank page…my words will write themselves across the lines…there is nothing else there…it is empty and white except for my words…"

The muscles in Claire's arms relaxed, her fingers loosened their grip on the armrests. She felt herself falling, but made no attempt to slow the descent – falling through blackness like Alice down the rabbit hole –falling until she reached the cushioned bottom of a deep well.

"Good, good," Mark's voice reminded her of her mothers when she had sung nursery rhymes to help her go to sleep. "Are you there yet, Claire?"

"Yes. I'm there." She felt irritated at the question, a flash of anger illuminating the chamber in which she was trapped. In its light, she saw a body sprawled across the floor. Its mouth was gaping open, its large dead eyes were staring up into the nothingness. This was not her safe place, but somewhere frightening, somewhere she had been before and never wanted to visit again.

"I don't want to be here," she screamed, the words reaching Mark as a whisper. "I don't want to be here. Get me out!"

"Claire, I can't hear you," Mark's voice was a lifeline out of this nightmare.

"I don't want to be here. Let me out!"

"Claire, I still can't hear you. Where are you, Claire?" A voice broke through the hypnotic fog, but it was not Mark's.

"Let me out, Daddy. I don't want to be here. I'm scared." This was not the voice of a grown woman, Mark realized, but of a girl, a frightened little girl.

"Daddy, I promise I will be good. Please, let me out. It's dark. I don't want to be here!" Claire was near hysteria. Her breathing quickened as she rubbed one hand violently across her chest.

Mark asked again, "Claire, where are you?"

"You know where I am. You put me here…please, let me out! I don't want to be here. Please, Daddy…" Claire wailed.

"O.K., O.K., it's all right. I'm here Claire. It's Mark." Now alarmed, he knew he had to rescue his client from whatever hell she was now experiencing. "I'm going to count backwards from ten. When I reach one, you will open your eyes. Ten, nine, eight…"

Claire clung to each number, as to the rungs of a ladder lowered into the pit, holding onto each sound, afraid her grip would weaken and she would disappear forever into this torment, so far removed from her own safe world.

"One." With Mark's last word, Claire opened her eyes. Blinded momentarily by the lamp on the table beside her, she struggled to keep them from closing. As her vision adjusted, Mark slowly came into focus.

At first, she was comforted by the familiar face, the eyes a visible sign of his concern. But as his features began to sharpen, anger pushed any relief she felt aside. How could someone who claimed to care about her force her down to such a torturous place? She was aware of a rumble in her stomach, the constriction of her throat, a reverse peristalsis, as all the hurt and indignation that she could normally suppress, was hurled upwards to spew out of her mouth.

"You don't care about me. You're just like all the others…You want me to be crazy so you can control my mind." Claire was standing now. "I killed someone yesterday. Do you hear?" She took a step towards Mark who was still seated. "I killed someone. He was real. He tried to help me and I killed him. Because that's what I do best."

"Claire, calm down." Mark reached up to pat her shoulder.

"Don't you touch me," Claire backed up, knocking over her chair, then started towards the door.

"I don't need you. Do you hear me?" Claire pointed a finger menacingly in Mark's direction. He was visibly shaken by this violent outburst and the demonic look on his client's face.

"Claire, wait, I was only…" but his words were erased by the slam of the office door and the sound of her footsteps as she ran down the hall. "Claire, I do care…" but the hall was empty. No one heard his words as they echoed off the walls.

Mark moved quickly across his office to the window that looked out onto a typical urban scene of tall buildings separated by thin strips of asphalt and concrete. He held his breath, waiting for his client to appear on the sidewalk below.

Every human fiber in his body was screaming at him to follow her, to bring her back to the safety of his presence, a padded cell against which she could flail and not be further harmed. When Claire finally appeared walking unsteadily towards the bus stop, Mark felt as if his heart would explode with fear and compassion for the frail woman. Where was she going in such a frantic hurry? But, before he had time to speculate, a bus pulled up and opened its door in front of a line of people that now included Claire.

As the door closed behind her, Mark sighed deeply and turned away from the window, shuffled back to his chair and sank down into its leather cushions. For several moments, he replayed in his mind the session with Claire. As he had at the diner, Mark felt they had been on the brink of a psychological breakthrough, one it had taken six months of therapy to reach.

When they first started meeting, Mark had assumed her depression was situational, and, thus, understandable. Who wouldn't take an emotional nosedive after such devastating losses as Claire had experienced? But, despite his best efforts to draw her out, to explore experiences in her childhood that might account for her prolonged and stubborn illness, he had gotten nowhere. Claire only wanted to talk about the baby's death, about David's desertion, assuring him that her childhood had been quite normal and happy and that her parents had always been supportive and caring.

Mark believed her and allowed Claire to focus on the events preceding the start of therapy. After only a few sessions, he had begun to tire of hearing the repetitive details of her various miscarriages and the loss of her child. More than once, he had struggled to suppress a yawn, hoping she hadn't noticed, and, in truth, began to tire of her endless whining. In his mind, he placed her in the category of a lonely woman in need of male companionship and sympathy, even if she did have to pay for the privilege.

Their next session, which had taken place at the diner, had renewed his interest in her case. Claire had opened a crack in the lid of her tightly locked psyche, enough to give Mark hope that, indeed, this woman's problems were complex and multi-layered, a challenge to any clinician worth his salt. He had looked forward to their next meeting and was delighted when she had called for an appointment before the scheduled time.

And, as he had hoped, this session had picked up where the last one left off –with the same emotional intensity. She had seemed open and vulnerable, the perfect state of mind to respond to hypnotic suggestion –a skill he had learned in school and had little chance to practice since.

It had been so easy. Even Mark was surprised by how quickly she had "gone under." As her breathing and heart rate slowed, his had quickened with the promise of insight into her childhood, possibly leading to a cure, a notch in his professional belt.

But, this was where things had seemed to fall apart. Mark reached up and rubbed his eyes and tight forehead at the memory of Claire's stricken face, her twisted mouth, out of which the voice of a terrified child had pleaded to be let out of wherever his soft words had sent her.

She had called him "Daddy." It was clear that Claire had been successful in hiding some terrible event in her childhood, perhaps, even, a suppressed memory of child abuse. Mark pressed his forefingers against his eyes, kicking himself for not seeing through her subterfuge sooner, before it was too late, before his attempt at hypnosis had backfired, sending his client fleeing from his office to God knows where, to do God knows what.

"I will never forgive myself if something happens to her. Never." Mark reached down and opened the bottom drawer of his desk, for Claire's file. He seemed to recall she had a sister and thought it might be a good idea to phone her and, however embarrassing, inform her of Claire's state of mind.

Just then, there was a soft knock on his door. Mark rubbed his face quickly with his sleeve and tucked his shirttail back inside his pants as he moved towards the door, convinced Claire had returned...that she was safely back in his protective care.

"Am I late?" A middle-aged woman stood in the doorway, hesitating, perplexed when her therapist did not immediately invite her into his office.

"We did have a session scheduled today?" she inquired.

Mark drew in a breath and tried to smile as he answered, "Why, yes, Mrs...er...Bowen. Please come in." He stood aside as she passed into the office.

"I'll be right back. I just need to freshen up," he said.

Mrs. Bowen pursed her lips and glanced at her watch before sitting in the chair opposite Mark's desk. She was puzzled when she heard his footsteps going down the hall towards the stairwell instead of the restroom.

In a few minutes, he returned and sat at the desk, pulled out a file from the drawer, and opened it in front of him without looking down.

"Now, where were we?" His words were not directed at his present client but towards the window where a fat pigeon was settling into a corner of the sill for a morning nap.

Chapter XI

Claire pushed open the exit door at the base of the stairwell. The bright morning light was intensified by her tears and she stumbled on the doorsill onto the rough concrete, scraping her hands and bruising her knees.

Ignoring the pain, she stood up and quickly surveyed the sidewalk, which was empty save for a group of people standing at the corner a few yards away. Mercifully, no one seemed to notice her —their attention focused on a city bus that had just pulled up.

Claire took her place at the back of the line and tried to wait patiently until it was her turn to climb aboard. Despite the stiffness in her knees, she lifted one foot to the bottom step and grabbed the handrails to pull herself up the remaining steps to the landing. She looked down at the meter, at the slit in its top, unable to comprehend its purpose, until the driver barked angrily, "Pay your fare, lady."

Claire glanced up at him with puffy, bloodshot eyes. The driver, a middle-aged man with a slight paunch above his leather belt, scowled back at her.

"Pay your fare or get off the bus."

Claire jammed her hand down inside her purse, fingering its contents. She brought out a handful of coins, two paper clips and a rubber band. Her hand shook, sending several of the coins spilling out onto the floor.

"Oh, I'm so sorry," she apologized to the driver who cursed in exasperation.

"Fifty cents, lady…two quarters. Drop in two quarters or get off my bus."

The coins had rolled in several directions, under the dash and the first row of seats. Claire bent down to retrieve them, winced as her knees touched the floor. One of the coins had become wedged in the small gap where the flooring met the side wall of the bus and Claire couldn't make it budge.

"That's it. I can see you hit the bottle early this morning. Now get off and go dry out somewhere else."

Claire, still groping for the coins, felt herself suddenly jerked to standing by the driver who held her arm tightly at the elbow, steering her towards the exit steps. He was a tall man and she had no strength to resist him. She grabbed the handrails to keep from falling and had descended two steps when she heard a soft tremulous voice behind her.

"Here's your fifty cents." It was the voice of an elderly woman followed by the clink of two coins as they slid down to the bottom of the meter. The driver loosened his grip on her arm, cursing under his breath.

"O.K. Go find a seat and be quick about it. You've already put me five minutes behind schedule. Go sit down!"

Claire turned and pulled herself back up to the landing, then took a few steps towards the back of the bus, surveying the seats and their occupants. She wanted to find the woman who had paid her fare. Most of the passengers were either absorbed in reading the paper or staring out of the window, as if deliberately avoiding looking at her. Claire felt her face redden as she started down the aisle.

She slid into an empty seat, three rows behind the driver, beside a small elderly woman wearing a flowered dress and hat decorated with a few plastic flowers. She did not seem to notice when Claire sat down, but stared straight ahead, her mouth a tight line, her hands neatly folded on top of a leather purse.

Once Claire had settled herself, the woman unclasped her bag, pulled out a white tissue, and handed it to Claire, still without looking her way or speaking a word.

Claire took the tissue, examined it as she had the coins, as if she had no idea of its purpose. Just then, a tear dropped onto the front of her shirt and Claire reached up to feel her face, surprised by the wetness on her cheeks and below her nose. She brought the tissue up and dabbed at her eyes, sniffing softly into its fold before wadding it up into a ball that she held tightly in her fist.

"Thank you…that was so kind," she spoke to the older woman. But, her seatmate turned away from her and looked out the window at the passing buildings and pedestrians on the sidewalk, a gesture Claire interpreted as a sign of disapproval.

Suddenly aware of how she must appear, Claire tried to smooth back her loose hair, still clutching the tissue in one hand. She glanced at the woman before looking past her to the street beyond.

The bus had stopped again. Claire watched as a pair of older men, talking loudly and waving their hands at each other, reached a glass door and disappeared inside. She recognized the door, could barely make out the outline of several heads through the smudged plate glass windows on either side.

Claire sprang up at the same time the driver closed the door and brought his foot down on the accelerator.

"Stop!" she called. "I want to get off here." The driver slammed on the brakes, sending Claire careening to the front of the bus, bracing herself with both hands against the flat windshield. She drew them away quickly leaving two oily prints on the glass. The driver retrieved a red, dirty cloth from the pocket beside his seat and reached over to clean away the marks with one hand, opening the bus door with the other.

"Get off and good riddance," he spoke to Claire as she stepped down towards the door. At the bottom step, she turned to look back at the old woman who had been sitting beside her. She waved to get her attention, wanting to thank her for kindness, but the woman sat stonily looking the other way.

"Get off lady or I'll call the cops," the driver enunciated each word carefully, barely concealing his burning anger.

His words pushed Claire down to the street. She stepped up onto the sidewalk just as the door behind her shut with a whoosh and the bus pulled away with the roar of an angry bull.

Claire grabbed onto the lamppost to stop herself from being sucked back into the roadway. Her heart was racing, her breath coming in shallow gulps. She clung to the pole and closed her eyes to shut out the spinning world and made herself take several deep breaths.

When she felt her pulse slowing down, she became aware of the sounds of cars and trucks passing behind her. She could hear the click of different kinds of heels on the sidewalk in front. With her last deep breath, she inhaled the enticing aroma of frying burgers and her stomach tightened.

"I'm starving," she spoke out loud, scanning her memory for the last time she had eaten. It had probably been the night before, when her landlord had knocked on the door, waking her from a troubled sleep. Complaining about rats, he had shoved the still warm bag of food into her hands and closed the door behind him before she could say a word. Her brain still foggy from sleep, Claire could not resist opening the bag to examine its contents and was delighted to find a generous serving of what must have been Mrs. Dulaney's homecooked lasagne. Even so, she had only been able to manage a few bites before fatigue overcame her need for sustenance. Forgetting to put the rest of the food in the refrigerator, she collapsed onto the bed and fell back easily into her unsettling dreams. The next morning, she had been in too much of a hurry to reach Mark's office to bother with breakfast, and now the tantalizing smells beckoned to her empty stomach.

The door to the diner opened again and a gray-haired man and woman emerged. Claire watched as, once on the sidewalk, they turned for a farewell kiss. Something inside her, her heart maybe, contracted at the way they looked into each other's eyes before turning and hurrying off in different directions down the street.

Claire walked over to the glass door until she was close enough to see the dirty finger marks around the handle. Shifting her body weight to pull it open, she braced the door with one foot until she could slip over the threshold and into the dim interior.

The smell was overpowering, the oil-saturated air coating the insides of her nostrils and throat. For a horrifying second, she thought she might wretch and grabbed onto the back of the nearest booth until the nausea passed. Her hand grazed the hair of the seat's occupant, a neatly coifed woman who turned to glare at Claire through her thickly lined and shadowed eyes.

Claire pulled her hand away and put her head down, focusing on the dirty tile floor, and was comforted by its familiar pattern. She could hear music coming from the jukebox in the corner —that, and the clatter of dishes from the kitchen above the drone of a dozen or so voices.

"Two specials –hold the gravy this time." Claire raised her eyes at the sound of the waitress' gravelly voice and found her friend leaning through the pick-up window to shout her order at the unseen cook. Claire started walking towards an empty stool at the counter, then changed her mind, and headed back to the same booth beside the jukebox that she and Mark had shared in what seemed a lifetime ago.

The gray and white Formica top was littered with the remnants of a meal: a half-eaten BLT beside a wilted piece of lettuce, a lipstick stained coffee cup, and a cigarette butt in the glass ashtray. Claire slid into the booth trying not to gag on the stench coming from the ash, hoping it wouldn't evoke another constriction of her empty stomach.

Instead, she studied the soft neon lights of the jukebox, the pulsing glint from the record that was spinning inside. She did not recognize its tune, a country song that she had never heard, a sad lament of betrayal and hurt and lost love.

So engrossed was she in this sorrowful tale, Claire did not notice the waitress' presence and was startled by her voice.

"Well, hi, Hon, I remember you," the lined face looked down at her. The waitress was wearing the same uniform, the same food-stained apron. This time, an unlit cigarette rested between her ear and scalp.

"You was in here with that cute hunk," she winked down at Claire, nudging her shoulder with the tip of a long, red-polished nail.

Claire blushed with embarrassment, but could not help smiling back at the kind woman.

"Yes, yes, I was. But I think you got the wrong idea…" Claire felt the need again to clarify her relationship to Mark.

"Never you mind, Hon, I see he's not with you today. So, I'll just shut up about him. Heh, you look like you've been through the wringer."

Claire brought a hand to her face, which was dry, and pulled away several strands of hair that were stuck to her cheek.

"Was he mean to you, Hon?" the waitress patted Claire's shoulder then leaned down to look directly into Claire's eyes. Before Claire could answer, the waitress reached into her apron pocket and pulled out a folded menu that she spread out on the table in front of Claire.

"I ain't met a man yet that was worth my tears. What you need is a good hot meal. Let me clear this stuff away and I'll be back to get your order." The waitress stacked the dirty plates, cup, and utensils on one hand and, with the other, gave the table a swipe using a wet, soiled cloth that seemed to have materialized from nowhere. Then, she left as quickly as she had appeared.

Claire stared down at the lines of beaded moisture left by the cloth. She lifted the menu from the table to keep the wetness from soaking through. The words seemed to rearrange themselves before her eyes –the letters forming syllables she could not pronounce, much less understand. But, it didn't matter. She knew what she wanted.

"A hamburger, no pickles, fries, and a chocolate milkshake," Claire told the waitress when she had returned with her order pad.

"You go, girl. In my experience, ain't nothing like a good meal to chase away the blues. I'll be back in a jif…"

Claire smiled at the woman's words as she watched her hurry away. There it was again, that same pluck she had seen before –that same ability to standup to life's problems and shove them right back in its face. Maybe, if she stuck around this woman long enough, she could become strong, too.

A new record fell down onto the turntable beside her with a soft thud. Claire turned and watched as the arm swung around, gently placing the needle in the first groove. As the song began, Claire recognized a strong female voice asserting something about boots and walking. The end of each line was punctuated by three drumbeats, that were sharp enough to leave an imprint on someone's back, Claire mused.

She closed her eyes, tapped the tabletop with her fingers in time to the music, feeling safe and happy. Welcome warmth flowed down to the tips of her fingers, down to the ends of her toes, which tapped the rhythm on the dirty floor.

"That's it," she said to herself. "I just need some boots." The last sentence was spoken out loud just as the waitress set down the heavy plate in front of Claire.

Claire blushed as the waitress winked.

"You're right, honey. That's what you need…some pointy-toed boots." She brought her hand up to shield her mouth from the view of the other customers. "Then you got to learn to kick'em where it hurts, if you know what I mean."

The waitress smiled broadly, patted Claire's shoulder, then hurried off. Claire stared down at her meal, then straight ahead to the blank wall across from her. An image began to appear. She saw the outline of a man, doubled over and holding his crotch. At first, she couldn't see his face…but, gradually, the features, which were pulled together in agony, emerged.

It was her father's face for a moment. Claire drew in a quick breath, was just about to scream when the image blurred and before fading completely, became David's face, then Mark's, and, finally, that of the angry bus driver. But, they were all distorted by pain…looking silly and pathetic.

Claire continued to stare at the wall until she could again see the cracks in the plaster and the lines of grease dripping down behind the seat. Steam from her food reached her nostrils and she was suddenly awake and hungrier than she had ever been in her life.

"Kick 'em where it hurts!" she said out loud before picking up her hamburger and attacking it with the same energy she had used to clean the kitchen years ago…the night her father left.

Chapter XII

Claire gulped her food, washing down huge bites of burger with the thick shake. She could feel her energy returning –power pulsing through her thin arms and legs. But, halfway through her meal, her stomach constricted again and she knew if she didn't stop eating immediately, the burger and fries would be back on the tabletop swimming in a pool of partially digested chocolate ice cream and milk.

When she was younger, such a feeling would send her to the bathroom where she would deposit her food in the toilet –then wash her face and swish out her mouth before rejoining her unsuspecting parents at the dinner table.

Determined to overcome this impulse, Claire pushed her plate away and closed her eyes as she inhaled and exhaled deeply. Several times she had to swallow hard to keep her stomach's contents from rising any higher in her throat.

Claire forced her mind away from the diner, away from the smells and sounds pervading the air around her. She tried to remember the sequence of events that had brought her back to this place. Mark's face came into focus —not drawn up in agony as his image on the wall had been —but softened, with gentle concern showing in his eyes.

As hard as she tried to hold onto that comforting memory, the face disappeared into a sudden blackness. Claire shivered and wrapped her arms around her chest, unable to open her eyes and escape from this frightening place.

"I don't want to be here," she spoke towards the greasy wall. "Let me out." By now her voice had drawn the attention of the other diners who turned to find the source of this anguished appeal with a mixture of concern and disgust.

"I don't want to be here," she spoke louder.

"Then leave," a male voice called derisively from the booth at the opposite end of the room.

Claire did not hear him. The darkness was now broken by a glint of light that grew, illuminating the chamber in which she was trapped. Sharp edges of leather poked up into her bottom. Wire hangers clanged overhead when she reached up for something to help her stand.

The light grew in size and intensity. With horror, she watched as the light illuminated another face —the mouth gaping open above a man's unshaven chin, blue eyes still and unblinking, staring back at her, mocking her, accusing her. The mouth began to move, "Ten, nine, eight…" it formed the words, but it was Mark's voice she heard.

"I don't want to be here. Please let me out." Claire's cry rose with each plea, echoing off of the chamber walls, as though it had no other place to go…no waiting ears that would absorb her anguish and rescue her from this hell.

"Wake up. It's O.K. I'm here." Mark's voice seemed far away, fading…Something touched her shoulder and she pulled away instinctively.

"Don't touch me," Claire screamed. "I don't need you. I don't need anyone. Don't touch me…"

Claire could feel someone's hands rubbing her arms, patting her cheeks, the backs of her own hands. It felt like a hundred hands were groping her. They were rough…like her father's the night he undressed her and threw her in the closet. She started to fall, as the floor of the chamber opened up beneath her.

"Help me," she wailed as she plummeted down, down. She could see the light above her grow smaller and dimmer as she continued to fall, the face looking down at her, sneering at her…the mouth moving, forming the word "murderer" but emitting no sound.

"Help me," she implored. But she knew her cries were futile, that she would fall forever, because no one who cared could hear her. Or was it just that no one was left that cared? She had pushed them all away…she would disappear off the face of the earth…and would not even be missed.

"Help me," she gave one more desperate attempt, then resigned herself to her fate. Her limbs began to relax, became fluid as if her bones had dissolved beneath her skin. "So, this is it," she mused as she gave in to the force of gravity pulling her down. "So this is what it's like to die. It's not so bad after all…after all…Oh!"

Claire gasped for breath as her body plunged into a pool of cold water. She flailed her arms and kicked her legs afraid her lungs would burst before she could find her way back to the surface. Through the wetness above her she could see a glow, and struggled with all her might to reach it. Claire suddenly, desperately, wanted to breathe again, to feel the ache of life. With a final surge of strength, she swam towards the light, broke through the surface, and opened her mouth, sucking in the warm, heavy air. Her limbs tingled, water dripped down her face and arms.

Her eyelids were still heavy, their lashes matted with the moisture that was running down her forehead. But, gradually, she managed to open them. As her focus cleared, she saw a figure seated in front of her. She could not make out who it was, but the blurred features of its face were familiar.

Claire felt a pressure on her now balled-up fists and looked down to find them covered by a man's calloused hands. They appeared strong, but not menacing. She did not pull away, but sat studying those hands. They were deeply lined, with dirt crusted beneath several broken nails.

More curious than afraid, Claire let her gaze work its way up the man's hand to his wrists. Shirt cuffs, dirty and frayed, poked out from beneath a wool coat. She followed the coat sleeves up to the shoulders then along the shoulders to the neck wrapped with a plaid scarf.

As she reached the man's face, a thrill of recognition rippled through her body. There was the scraggly chin, the mouth she had seen in her dream, not gaping open, but forming a faint smile. And those eyes, those blue-blue eyes, returning her gaze, were animate. She could make out a line in the skin between them, a "worry line" as her mother used to call it. The relief that flooded her limbs then was overpowering and she shut her eyes and began to float away...

"Stay here, now," a deep male voice commanded. "Don't leave us again, miss. We're here. It's O.K."

Claire was startled back to consciousness by a few drops of water flung into her face. "Come on now, Hon. Stay with us." She opened her eyes and looked up into the worried face of the waitress who was standing beside the booth holding a glass of water.

"Oh, thank you...thank you. I thought I'd killed him, you see —but you brought him to me and he's alive...he's alive." The waitress exchanged a wary glance with the man sitting across from Claire.

"Of course, he's alive, Hon," she patted the younger woman's shoulder, attempting to speak in an even tone so as not to upset her further.

"But, don't you see. I'm not crazy. He's real. I killed him and now he's alive. I'm not crazy after all." Claire's voice was high pitched, her words spilling out faster than she could pronounce them clearly.

"What's she saying?" a bass voice from the other side of the room bellowed through the thick air.

Claire heard him this time and used her arms to push herself up to standing, then turned, grabbing the back to the booth to brace herself. "I said, I'm not crazy." She spoke to the balding top of a man's head that poked up from behind the seat back.

"Well, ain't that a relief," he directed to his seatmates who joined him in laughter.

But, Claire didn't mind the laughter. She didn't mind the insult. She didn't mind the fact that she was sitting in a public place, covered with water, her hair flying out in all directions. For, sitting across from her was a man with the bluest eyes she had ever seen. He was alive and that was all that mattered.

Claire's arm brushed her plate as she reached over to touch the bristly cheek to assure herself that the man was really there. He drew back from her touch, but Claire didn't notice, nor did she notice his mouth as he whispered, "Dial 911," to the waitress who hurried off. Suddenly ravenous, Claire pulled her plate closer and picked up the remnants of her burger.

As she brought it to her mouth, she explained to the stranger, "I'm not crazy. Just hungry." With that, she stuffed the bread and meat into her mouth, chewing noisily before swallowing. She grabbed the glass and sucked up the rest of her milk shake, then took another breath, and turned to the waitress who had hurried back to her side, "You got to eat, you know…" Claire bit off the end of a french fry before completing her sentence, "if you want to live."

Chapter XIII

"Claire, honey, wake up. It's Nita. I'm here." Nita sat beside the hospital bed, rubbing her sister's cold, limp hand. She watched anxiously as Claire's eyelids began to flutter, then struggle to open.

"That's it, sweetie. You can do it…open your eyes."

Claire could hear Nita's voice from somewhere far away. She tried to move her mouth and respond, but it took such effort to overcome the heavy weight pressing down on her face and limbs that she gave up and let herself slide back down into her dream.

It had been such a wonderful dream, too, and so real. In it, she had finally found the stranger. He was not dead at all but sitting across from her, holding her hand, speaking to her. She touched the side of his face that had a pink glow. Music played in the background but she did not recognize the tune, was only aware of the joy she felt at finding him, proving she was neither a murderer nor a crazy person.

Someone else had been there, someone kind who had brought Claire food that tasted like the air —salty and greasy. Claire swallowed the saliva engendered by this memory of her last meal. It's bitterness caused her to gag, a convulsion deep in her throat squeezed her windpipe and she opened her mouth struggling for air to fill her aching chest.

"Help me," Claire screamed silently to the stranger before falling forward onto the table, her forehead cushioned by a pile of ketchup soaked french fries.

"Claire, Claire…I can't hear you honey. Wake up, now." Nita rubbed Claire's hand a little harder and reached over to pat her sister's face just as she opened her eyes and sat up, coughing and gasping.

Nita waited for her sister's breaths to become deep and even, for her eyes to lose the look of a frightened deer and focus.

"You gave us a scare," Nita stood and cupped Claire's face between her large soft hands, turning her sister's head so she could look directly into her eyes.

Claire blinked with an effort to clear the blurred image of Nita's face, that, at first, she was unable to recognize. Gradually, the face, now inches from her own, became that of someone she loved.

"Nita?" Claire moved her tongue and lips with difficulty.

"Yes, sweetie, it's me. I'm here," Nita drew back from Claire, sinking into her chair with relief, still clinging to Claire's hand.

"Don't ever pull a stunt like that again, you naughty girl," Nita teased, trying to conceal her concern. "Good thing I was on duty in the nursery when they brought you into the emergency room."

Emergency room? Nursery? Claire forced her gaze from Nita's face and let her eyes explore the room. The wall in front of her was covered with flowered paper. A window, its blinds drawn to block out the bright sunlight beyond, filled the end wall. Beside her bed, bags of fluid hung from several metal poles. Claire visually followed the lines connected to the bags as they crossed over the bed rails and disappeared into the back of her right hand.

"Where am I?" she croaked.

"In the hospital. Don't you remember? They brought you in yesterday." Nita smoothed back the hair that was matted on Claire's forehead. "You apparently choked. You were having lunch at some diner on Danvers Street. Lord knows what you were doing in that part of town."

A collage of images flashed in Claire's mind –a lit jukebox, a hamburger with several bites taken out of it, a woman's face above a dirty apron, a hand holding her own –a large hand, lined and dirty.

"Good thing your friend knew the Heimlich maneuver and acted quickly or you might not have made it."

The Heimlich? What is she talking about? Claire tried to remember the day before. What had she done? Where had she gone? What friends was Nita talking about? She didn't have any friends.

"They said you passed out right there at the table. You've still got ketchup in your hair." Nita took a washcloth from the bedside table, wet it in the water pitcher, and started dabbing at a crusty patch on Claire's scalp.

"What are you talking about?" Claire reached up and pushed Nita's arm away. Several drops of water had splashed onto her face and she was suddenly, completely awake. Another image formed in her mind —a water glass —someone was holding it and flicking water in Claire's face.

And she was back there again —at the diner - smothered by the smell of frying onions, listening to the music from the jukebox -something about boots - feeling the weight of the waitress' arm on her shoulder, and of someone's hand on her own -someone kind... someone with blue eyes.

Claire began to laugh and with a burst of energy, pulled Nita over. "Oh, Nita, it's so wonderful. I found him. He's alive. I touched his face."

Nita pushed Claire gently back onto the pillow, trying to calm her, afraid, in her frenzy, that she might pull the IV line out of her hand.

"O.K., sweetie. I'm sure you did. Now, just try and relax."

"No, you don't understand," Claire fought weakly to stay upright. "He's alive...and, and, I'm not crazy. He's called "the Duke," and I killed him, or I thought I'd killed him, but then I didn't, you see, and he saved my life —again —and I need to find him and thank him." She grabbed Nita's arm with such ferocity that Nita reached over with her free hand and punched the nurse's button.

"Of course you're not crazy. No one said you were. Just lie back now and rest…you need to rest."

Nita spoke in the same soothing tone she used for her fussy preemies -in a slow, rocking rhythm. She stroked her sister's hair. "Yes, the Duke. We'll find the Duke and tell him and the Queen, too."

Queen? What was Nita talking about? Claire was puzzled, but the effect of her sister's soothing voice and touch made her eyelids feel heavy again and she released the grip on Nita's arm and sank back onto the pillow, into a deep dreamless sleep.

Nita put her finger to her lips when the nurse entered the room, whispering, "It's O.K. She's asleep." The nurse tiptoed to the IV poles, checked the fluid level and rate of drip, then, satisfied, returned to the hall. Nita closed her own eyes, weary from her overnight vigil, relieved that Claire had survived the ordeal, but with a new concern over the state of her mind.

She had called Claire's therapist the night before. He had promised to look in on her and determine her emotional status. Nita wondered if Claire had finally gone over the edge…certainly her words sounded delusional…definitely not in touch with reality. She almost hoped the doctors would decide to keep Claire even after the physical danger had passed. Nita knew her sister needed help —more than she had the time or energy to give her. Maybe a few weeks on the psychiatric ward would finally pull Claire from the deep well in which she had lived since the baby's death.

Nita was startled from her reverie by the nurse's entrance. This time she was carrying a large glass vase of flowers, multi-colored blooms dotted with six cream-colored roses which she placed on the window ledge.

"Who brought those?" Nita asked the nurse as she crossed to the door. The bouquet looked expensive and Nita wracked her brain to think of someone in Claire's life rich enough to afford such a lovely arrangement. The nurse shrugged her shoulders and left the room.

"They must be from Mark," Nita mused. "How thoughtful." She was sure Claire's therapist had sent them, though, after staring at the white envelope wedged into a long plastic holder, Nita was overcome with curiosity. She walked across the room, glancing guiltily at Claire, who appeared to be sleeping peacefully, and retrieved the card.

The envelope was addressed simply, "To the lady in Rm. 212." Nita knew it couldn't be from Mark. Still reluctant to invade Claire's privacy, she looked over at her sister's face which, in sleep, was that of a little child…the same child she had watched over so many years ago. Nita had not seen Claire look so young and carefree for years, even when she was sleeping. Something or someone was responsible for this new sign of life in her sister and she was determined to find out just who he or she was.

Nita pulled the florist card from its envelope. Surrounded by a border of pink roses, the message read, "I still think you are pretty. Get well soon. -The Duke."

Chapter XIV

Nita sat down beside Claire's bed, still clutching the card. She knew she should feel relieved at this evidence of the existence of "The Duke," clearly not a figment of her sister's imagination. But, something about the whole situation disturbed her. She did not like the thought of a strange man insinuating himself into Claire's life.

She wondered if she should telephone David, though she doubted he would be of any help. He had called to speak to Fred a few months ago, to tell him of his plans to remarry, knowing his ex-brother-in-law would not simply hang up on him, the way he feared that Nita would. Fred had not asked any details, including where David and his bride planned to live. Nita had been irritated at her husband for asking no questions and for assuming that she would be the one to tell Claire.

Nita did not blame David for leaving her sister. She had liked David from the first day they met, Thanksgiving Day of Claire's senior year of college.

Nita had not been overly impressed by the other boys that Claire had dragged home on the weekends. She felt they were far too shallow and prone to partying to be suitable lifetime mates for her baby sister.

But, David had been different. Something about his face reminded her of their father's, though she had found the similarity more pleasant than disturbing. She liked the way he joined in the conversation at the table, laughed at the tales of Claire's childhood antics, the way he touched her sister's hand. After dinner on the family's traditional Thanksgiving walk, Nita had noticed a certain lightness in her sister's step and the ease with which the couple moved together, comfortable with each other's bodies.

Nita even envied Claire and David's passion for one another. By then, she and Fred merely exchanged a nightly kiss, anxious to catch a few hours of sleep before their noisy brood woke. She envied her sister's carefree college years, unencumbered by the demands of motherhood, something Nita had jumped into soon after leaving high school. She wondered what she had missed by marrying so young, even if it was to someone she loved. Perhaps she should have sampled single life instead of diving headfirst into her roles as wife and mother.

Their own mother had not been present for that particular Thanksgiving gathering. By then, she had remarried...this time to the lumpy looking, good-natured lawyer in the firm where she worked. When he had first asked her out, Mary had refused, but Nita and Claire felt it was time their mother got on with her life and urged her to accept if he asked again.

He had. After dating for only three months, the happy couple announced to their families their intentions to marry. A few weeks after the courthouse ceremony, attended by Nita, Claire, Fred and their new stepfather's grown son and his family, the groom whisked his bride off to life in a retirement community in St. Petersburg. From all reports, their mother was happier than she had ever been in her marriage to their father, as revealed in the few letters she sent north to her children.

Nita had been delighted at her mother's newfound happiness, but bore some resentment at suddenly becoming the matron of the family. Mary claimed that they could not afford the plane fare for a trip home, not even for holidays. But, Nita felt her mother was simply relieved to be away from people and places that reminded her of the many years spent locked in a miserable relationship and dealing with Claire's emotional problems.

Nita had decided not to call her mother about Claire's hospitalization, not until she could find out more from the doctors. She knew from experience that her mother would not offer any help, but merely worry.

Nita and Fred's home was now the unspoken site of all family gatherings, on both sides. That was why she readily agreed to Claire's including David that particular Thanksgiving. What was one more face at the table among all their own children, Fred's nieces and nephews, aunts and uncles?

The middle child of seven, David fit right into the mayhem. Nita was particularly impressed by his interest in the children, the way he teased them, joined in their outside games of tag, bounced the youngest ones on his knee while singing a rhyme.

"We're planning to have a dozen kids," David announced at Christmas that year. By then, it was obvious to everyone that Claire and David would marry, even though it was not yet official.

"A dozen and one," Claire corrected with a bright smile and hug of her future husband's broad shoulders.

It was difficult for Claire to concentrate on completion of her degree in Special Education, but Nita urged her to finish. They had decided on a small church wedding a month after graduation. Predictably, their mother had feigned illness two days before she was supposed to fly home for the ceremony, and Nita walked Claire down the short aisle. Nita had not been conscious of carrying any burden until, with the minister's final pronouncement, she felt suddenly light and free, the cloud of responsibility for her sister's wellbeing blown away with the sweet scent of lilies from the bridal bouquet.

After a honeymoon to Bermuda, Claire and David settled down in a small house several miles from Nita and Fred. David already had a job working for his father, helping to establish a branch of the family business in their city. Claire found a job teaching kids with disabilities at the elementary school a few blocks from their home.

The first two years of their life together seemed to fly by. They had decided to put off having a family until David's income would allow Claire to quit teaching and be a stay-at-home Mom. Claire became pregnant a month after stopping birth control. Nita could tell by the new spring in David's step and the tenderness in his eyes when he looked at his wife, that he was thrilled at the prospect of becoming a father, bouncing his own child on his knee instead of a nephew or cousin.

Claire, too, bloomed for awhile, until, in her third month, she began to spot, losing the baby a few days later. Claire had been crushed, but David was devastated. Still, assured by the doctor that there was no reason why they could not produce a healthy child, they had tried again.

This time, in the fourth month, the pregnancy again spontaneously terminated, and the physical and emotional ramifications of that second loss began to take its toll on the couple's relationship.

Feeling she had let her husband down, Claire drew into her self, even when it was physically safe for them to restart sexual relations. She refused to let David touch her. Angry and grieving himself, David had interpreted her actions as a rejection of him, a smear on his manhood.

At Nita's suggestion, they had gone to counseling. Within the safety of a neutral space and in the presence of an impartial arbiter, they had poured out their anger, fears, pain, and hurt. By the third session, they were back in each other's arms, renewing their love and willing to risk another attempt at becoming parents.

This pregnancy had lasted the entire nine months. After the fourth month, they told Nita and Fred the good news. Nita was thrilled for both of them, relieved to see the strengthening of their marital bond. Both Claire and David glowed with anticipation as each month passed. They decided not to learn the sex of the baby, choosing neutral colors for the nursery and fabric for the curtains. David had searched several lumberyards before finding the right wood with which to build the cradle. While Claire painted the nursery ceiling, she could hear the whir of David's electric saw through the open window and could barely wait to see his creation.

Everything had gone fine. Claire went into labor the day after she turned in her final grades for the school year. Nita and Fred joined them at the hospital, sitting anxiously in the waiting room, as David emerged periodically to give a report on the baby's progress. Claire seemed to stay on top of the contractions, refusing any pain medication so as not to compromise the baby's health.

"It's coming!" David had shouted from the labor room door, not wanting to risk leaving his wife or missing the miracle that was about to occur. Too many minutes elapsed before David finally emerged. Nita knew something was terribly wrong as soon as they saw his tearstained face. He had rushed right past them, his unseeing eyes staring straight ahead, staggering down the hall, touching the wall like a drunk trying not to fall down.

It was Nita who stayed with Claire that night, holding her, rocking her, avoiding her questions of when David would be back. She needed him so, needed the assurance of his love. She needed him to tell her it was not her fault that the baby had died.

But David had not come back to the hospital. Nita and Fred drove Claire home the next day. Nita put her sister to bed while Fred searched the house for David, finding him in a heap in the garage, his head resting on a canvas drop cloth that covered what appeared to be a piece of furniture. He had been asleep. Fred was reluctant to wake him, but when he touched David's shoulder, the grieving man had sprung up, greeted his brother-in-law cheerily and asked if he would like a glass of iced tea.

As Nita studied her sister's peaceful face, she remembered that first night home after the baby's death. Claire had slept fitfully, her features often drawn into a grimace. Sometimes she moaned or called out for David. But, again, her husband hadn't come. After eating only a few bites of the meal Nita had cooked, David had retreated to the garage where he slept until dawn.

The next morning, David joined Nita and Claire in the kitchen for breakfast, but neither he nor his wife spoke. Claire stared into her plate of eggs not even bothering to move the food around with her fork or pretending to take a bite. David ate everything on his plate, swallowed the last of his coffee, then left for work without a word of thanks or even acknowledgement that his sister-in-law was still there.

Nita had not been angry at him and began to feel some of his frustration when after several weeks, Claire made no attempt to resume cooking or housecleaning or even bathing or dressing herself.

Nita thought of David as she watched her sister sleep…she prayed he had found happiness and decided not to intrude upon his new life. Perhaps he would soon have a child of his own on the way…she hoped so.

Nita pulled the light blanket up around her sister's shoulders, stood and looked down at her still form, at the gentle rise of her chest as she breathed. With that peaceful image of Claire still in her mind, Nita walked out into the hall to call Fred. Good old dependable Fred.

Chapter XV

"Claire?" Mark whispered for fear of waking his client if she were in a deep sleep. Alarmed by her agitation at the end of their last session, he dared not risk provoking another such outburst just by his very presence.

Mark considered himself an astute practitioner, but had been completely unprepared for the extreme horror Claire seemed to experience while hypnotized and the violence of the anger directed towards him when brought back to consciousness. Hypnosis could sometimes be risky -he knew that from experience - but their last time together, at the diner, had been so productive and he felt that she was ready to delve even deeper into the underlying cause of her deep depression.

As he sat by her bedside, Mark could not shake the feeling that he was responsible for her being here, in the hospital. He studied her face, so peaceful in sleep, and chuckled softly, imagining her reaction to being seen with her tangled, unkempt hair twirling out in all directions across the pillow.

Claire looked so young, so vulnerable –almost like a child -the child she must have been before illness and circumstance robbed her of her innocence and youth. Mark's throat tightened as he recalled her accusatory words, "You don't care about me…You just want to control me –like all the others."

Was he like all the other doctors and therapists that had been in Claire's life? Did he really care about her wellbeing or was she just another problem to be solved, another interesting challenge -not a person, but a case study to be presented at the next psychology conference? And if he cared at all, was it enough?

Filled with remorse and shame at not being able to answer his own questions, Mark stood and leaned over the sleeping figure, kissing her gently on the forehead. A tear dropped onto her cheek and he carefully blotted it with his shirt cuff before running his sleeve across his own wet face.

"I do care, Claire," his words were barely audible, but without opening her eyes, Claire turned her head towards Mark. Her lips moved but he could hear no sound. He waited a few minutes more before walking towards the door.

"I know."

Was it his imagination, what he longed to hear, or had Claire actually spoken? He turned quickly and looked back towards the bed. The only movement he could see was the rhythmic rise and fall of the still sleeping woman's chest. Mark stood a moment more then tiptoed quietly out of the room.

"Did you talk to her?" Nita stood outside the doorway, an anxious expression on her face.

"No, she was sleeping. I didn't want to disturb her," Mark paused and examined his shoes.

"Is she going to be alright?"

Again, Mark avoided Nita's eyes, focusing on the elevator door at the end of the hallway.

"I don't know. I'll call on her later this evening. Given the state of mind she was in yesterday, I'm sure the doctors will not want to release her without consulting me." Mark spoke to the poster hanging on the wall above Nita's head. "In any case, when she does leave here, she shouldn't be alone, at least for a few days."

"Fred and I can take care of her," Nita sighed, puzzled by Mark's evasive behavior. "Heaven knows we've done it before. And to be honest, Mark, I'm concerned for her safety. She keeps talking about some stranger who saved her life, "the Duke"…she's obsessed with him."

"I know. She told me that she had killed him during our last session. Of course, I thought she was hallucinating," Mark glanced towards the door of Claire's room. "I didn't take her seriously. Maybe if I had…" His voice trailed off. For a moment, Nita thought he was going to cry.

"It's the strangest thing –this "duke" fellow sent her some flowers. I guess he's real after all. But, it still gives me the creeps. He could be dangerous." Nita grabbed Mark's shirtsleeve, hoping to force him to look at her, instead, he pulled away, checked his watch and started towards the elevator.

"All the reason for her not to be alone. I'll call later, it's best for her to sleep now."

Nita watched him walk away, glad there was someone else looking out for her baby sister. She sometimes fantasized that Mark and Claire would fall in love and marry, could imagine them standing together at the altar, gazing into each other's eyes as they spoke their vows. He would be dressed in a white shirt and khaki pants, Claire in a flowing dress, her hair artfully arranged by Nita in a bun surrounded by real orchids. Nita leaned against the wall and closed her eyes just as the elevator door shut behind Mark. Why was life so hard for Claire? Oh, if she could find just a little bit of happiness…

"Excuse me, Ma'am."

Nita, startled by this strange voice, opened her eyes, bringing her pocketbook up instinctively as a shield. Before her stood a tall, thin man. She could not guess his age. His face was hidden behind a scraggily beard, long greasy curls spilling onto his shoulders. Dressed for a winter day, she counted several layers of clothing beneath his long overcoat.

His sudden appearance was alarming, but what kept Nita from running for help were his eyes −the bluest eyes she had ever seen −piercing, yet incredibly gentle. They were not the red, bleary eyes of a drunk, the unfocused eyes of the bums she passed by quickly on the sidewalk.

Somewhat mesmerized, she still managed to step back, hugging her purse to her chest.

"I didn't mean to startle you, ma'am," the man spoke apologetically, but still boldly looking directly at Nita. "I just wondered if you were related to the lady in this room." He pointed towards Claire's door.

"Yes, I'm her sister...but who are you? What do you want with Claire? She's ill. She's sleeping." Nita positioned herself between the stranger and the doorway, raising herself up to her full height, filling the space between the door jams.

"Claire...is that her name? It's lovely, it suits her... Claire..." he repeated several times more as if testing the sound, then smiled broadly.

Nita was again startled by the whiteness of his teeth. They were straight and even, no brown blotches from nicotine or gaps from teeth lost in a street fight.

"Who are you and what do you have to do with my sister?" Nita shook herself menacingly like a puffed-up turkey.

"Oh, I'm, sorry. Let me introduce myself. My name is Daniel, but my friends call me 'the Duke'."

Nita's mouth dropped open, her mind reeling from this revelation. She could not reconcile this man's appearance, his ragged clothes and days-old beard with his cultured voice. For that matter, he did not look like anyone with enough money to send the bouquet of flowers that was sitting on the window ledge in Claire's room. Blue eyes or not, she was not about to let this odd fellow anywhere near her sleeping sister.

"Did you send those flowers?" Nita's tone was that of a schoolteacher to a naughty child.

"She didn't like them? I picked out the prettiest blooms in the florist shop...but, if they're not right," the Duke paused a moment, as if in deep thought. "I knew I should have gotten daisies. Anyone named Claire must have daisies."

He took one step towards the door before being pushed back by Nita's strong outstretched arm. "Oh, no you don't. She's sleeping and I don't want her disturbed. Claire really appreciates the flowers, so thoughtful of you."

Nita was beginning to get nervous. She didn't know how to keep this man away from her sister without provoking him. He could be crazy or carrying a concealed weapon. She pushed these last panicky thoughts down and stated politely but firmly, "Thank you so much for coming by and for the flowers. It was very kind of you. Now, please leave..."

The Duke finished the end of her sentence, "before you call security?" He had heard it many times before and was no longer offended when people reacted to him with fear and distrust. In fact, it fit nicely into his need to confuse, to burst people's stereotypical opinion...their tendency to judge the proverbial book by its cover.

"Please give m'lady, Claire, my regards. It was a pleasure." Before Nita knew what was happening, the Duke bent forward, took her hand and kissed its back, then turned gracefully, his full coat swinging around him like a Cavalier's cape.

Nita pulled her hand away and gasped, could not breathe for a moment as she stared at the dignified figure walking away with his shoulders pushed back and head held high. He paused before the exit door, turned and tipped an imaginary hat in Nita's direction, then disappeared so quickly down the stairwell, she wondered if he had been real at all…or merely a figment of her weary imagination.

"I can't find my brush." When Nita entered the room she found Claire out of bed, standing in front of the table. One hand was thrust inside the top drawer, the other was held in midair, straining against her IV line. She seemed to take no notice of the gap in the back of her hospital gown. Nita winced at this unwanted glimpse of her sister's flat bottom and thin legs.

"Claire, honey, you need to lie down. I'll find your brush." Nita moved quickly, grasping her sister's shoulders from behind and steering her firmly towards the bed. Claire's weak protest was no match for her sister's maternal instinct. She sat on the edge of the mattress, but did not recline.

"Claire, you need your rest. You've been through such an ordeal," but Claire managed to stay upright, planting her feet squarely on the floor and bracing herself on either side with her hands.

"Nita, I feel fine, really. I feel great, in fact. I want to go home. I need to go home and feed Max. He'll starve if I'm not there…" Claire's voice rose with concern. She tried to stand back up, but lost her balance, falling back onto the bed and then giving into gravity as her head sank back on the pillow.

"Max is fine. Fred went by last night to feed him. He was sleeping on the windowsill as usual. Fred said he lifted his head, yawned, then went right back to sleep. You know cats, they're quite self-sufficient." Nita pulled a brush from her large handbag.

"Here, sweetie. Sit up a little and I'll try to do something with this mess."

Claire propped herself up on her elbows, dismayed at how weak she felt. Her arms trembled with the effort and her neck was barely able to keep her head up to resist Nita's brushstrokes. She closed her eyes as Nita teased out each tangle. The touch of her sister's hands felt like a caress. She thought of all the times she had relied on her sister to be both comfort and strength just to make it from one day to the next.

"Nita," Claire spoke softly, her eyes still closed.

"What, honey?" Nita did not miss a beat.

"I'm sorry."

"Sorry for what?" Nita continued the rhythmic brushing even though she had long since smoothed the unruly hair.

"For everything…for being so…weak." Claire swallowed to clear what felt like an obstruction in her throat. "You've always had to take care of me. It's not fair. You have your own family to worry about. You don't need another…" Claire struggled to find a word to complete her thought, but was interrupted by the sound of a nasally voice coming from the intercom in the hall.

"Dr. Wright, please call extension 924."

Nita stopped brushing and studied her sister's face. Only two days ago, Claire had pushed her away, declaring she needed no one's help. Nita had been angry and hurt. When she got word of Claire's ER admission, a part of her wanted to just walk away. Claire had made it quite clear that she did not want Nita in her life, so why come to her rescue? It would serve her right. But Nita's nature, her role as caregiver, had not allowed her to sustain this bitterness for long.

"Claire, honey, it's O.K. We're family, remember? I'll be here as long as you need me." Claire sat up and grasped Nita's hand with her own.

"But, it's different now. I can be strong." Claire squeezed Nita's fingers until they started to ache. "You'll never have to take care of me again." Claire punctuated each word of the last sentence with a stronger grip of her sister's hand. Nita struggled to pull it away before Claire inflicted permanent damage.

"Of course you can be strong, Sis," Nita laughed as she shook her throbbing fingers. "A little too strong, if you ask me." Claire looked blankly at her sister, then made the connection between her own actions and her sister's words. Nita's growing laughter was contagious and Claire joined in.

"Oh, Nita," Claire hiccuped then threw her arms around her broad, soft sister. Nita returned the embrace and together they laughed until the bed started shaking and the nurse popped her head in to make sure her ward was all right.

They held each other tightly until the laughter turned to sobs…this time, tears of relief and joy.

Together, they rocked back and forth until Claire went limp in her sister's arms. Thinking she was asleep again, Nita released her sister's embrace and lowered her gently back onto the pillow.

"Nita?"

"Yes, sweetie?"

"Will you take me with you to rock the premature babies?"

Nita did not know how to answer this unexpected request. She did not know if her sister was strong enough physically or emotionally to handle those tiny beings. But this was the first time in months that Claire had expressed interest in anything outside herself.

"Maybe tomorrow...maybe tomorrow..." Nita kept her vigil until she was certain Claire was asleep, then rose stiffly and walked to the door, pausing to look back at her sister's peaceful face. She knew Claire was far from well, but this last interchange filled Nita with a hope she had not thought was possible for her sister's full recovery. She couldn't wait to tell Fred.

"Maybe tomorrow," she said, blowing a kiss and glancing guiltily across the room at the flowers which, to her relief, Claire had not yet noticed. Nita knew it would take at least a good night's sleep and some well-rehearsed words before she could explain their presence. That, and a little white lie, she thought to herself as she shuffled wearily down the hall, unconsciously rubbing the back of her hand, the same hand the Duke had so valiantly kissed.

Chapter XVI

Claire woke the next morning with a clear head and an unfamiliar feeling of anticipation. The room glowed from the morning sun. She glanced over towards the window expecting to see Max' silhouette. Instead, a large bouquet of flowers stood on the window ledge.

Flowers? Who had sent her flowers? And where was Max? Claire sat up quickly. The IV cord became tangled in the bed rail.

"Ouch," Claire looked down at her hand. The world began to right itself as she remembered she was not at home.

"I bet they're from Nita and Fred," she mused, "or maybe Mark."

Tears filled her eyes as she thought of the three persons dearest to her. She had treated them all so badly.

"I don't deserve this…" she spoke out loud, just as a white-coated doctor strode into the room, followed by several bleary-eyed medical students with stethoscopes draped around their necks.

"You don't deserve what?" The gray-haired physician opened the chart that was cradled in his arm. "It says here, Miss, you deserve a big breakfast followed by our house special, a luxurious sponge bath administered by a handsome orderly."

Claire blushed at being caught talking to herself and could not suppress a smile in the presence of such good humor.

"That sounds wonderful, but I'd rather take a bath at home. I'm feeling so much better." The doctor raised his eyebrows. "Really," she hastily added.

"We'll see about that. The nurse will be in a minute to draw some blood. If everything comes back normal…" The doctor paused as he read a note on Claire's chart. "We also need to get the all-clear from Dr. Farrell. Has he been into see you today?"

Dr. Farrell? Claire could not recall having seen anyone by that name. Still, it sounded familiar.

"Oh, you mean Mark. No, I don't think he's been here since I was admitted. But I'm sure he'll tell you I'm perfectly fine."

"Apparently he has been here and was concerned about your state of mind when they brought you in. I understand you gave the ER folks a run for their money."

Claire blushed again. She had no memory of the few hours spent downstairs. She only knew what Nita had told her the day before. She also knew it was important to stay calm if she hoped for an early release.

"I didn't know what I was saying…must have been a lack of oxygen from choking."

The doctor was still absorbed in her chart. "Says here you have a history of depression and an eating disorder." He looked up, then, his face grim. "How can we be sure you won't starve yourself again?"

"Please," Claire was dismayed by her childish whine. "You have to let me go. I have something I must do. I promise to eat."

"Let me see what Dr. Farrell says after he speaks to you. Do you have someone to stay with for a few days? Not that I don't trust you." This new twinkle in the doctor's eye brought another blush to Claire's face.

"Just remember, Claire, you have to eat if…"

"I know, I know," Claire rolled her eyes, was about to finish his sentence when the doctor and his entourage whipped around and vanished from the room.

Claire recalled the first time she had heard that admonition from the psychiatrist at the hospital years ago. For her, it had been a joke, with emphasis on the "if." She had been so pleased at how easily she fooled the therapists and doctors, pretending to want to live just to get out of the hospital, when secretly she hadn't cared if she lived or died.

A more recent memory came to the surface, that of Nita sitting across from her at a table, speaking the same admonition. Claire's response then had also been defiant, as she balled up her food and threw it in the trash can.

A moment later, a nurse that she had not seen before entered the room carrying a plastic container holding several glass test tubes. "Just need to get a sample. It won't take a minute." Claire barely noticed the needle prick, her mind still focused on her silly gesture and the surprised look on Nita's face. It seemed so childish now.

After the nurse had finished and left the room, Claire turned towards the window. She sat up, swung her legs over the side of the bed, grabbed the IV pole and walked over to get a closer look at the flowers. She studied each bloom, each unique design, the infinite detail of every petal, stem and leaf. Tucked in among the yellows and pinks were several small blue cornflowers, the color of someone's eyes —someone kind and caring.

Claire renewed her resolve to get out of the hospital, to find the Duke and thank him for saving her life. All that stood in her way were a blood test and a good report from Mark.

She had dreamed of Mark the night before. There had been a kiss and something wet on her cheek. He had spoken to her and she had replied, but despite her best efforts, the words remained illusive.

Poor Mark. Claire flinched at the memory of their last session. She had accused Mark of not caring and had pushed him away just as she had Nita. Claire did not know what she had said exactly, but her words must have been harsh, given the stricken look on his face before she ran from his office. Maybe the flowers were from Mark, dear Mark.

"Good morning, Sis." Nita sailed into the room. Her ample body and obvious good mood filled the small space. "I met Dr. Wright in the hall. He said they might release you today." Nita joined Claire at the window, trying to direct her sister's attention away from the Duke's bouquet.

"Let me look at you." Nita cupped Claire's face between her hands. "Yep, she's back. That's the Claire I know." Nita pulled Claire's head down and planted a wet kiss on her forehead. "The Claire I've missed for so long."

Claire was a bit puzzled by her sister's fuss. As far as she knew, she had not gone anywhere. But, she was pleased to be back in her sister's good graces and made a silent vow to never hurt her again.

"Nita, you and Fred shouldn't have." Claire bent down to smell one of the rosebuds.

Nita fidgeted with the clasp of her purse, fingered her necklace. Over breakfast that morning, Fred had urged his wife to tell Claire the truth, to treat her as an adult for a change. But, Nita still felt that there was a time and a place for everything and that she would reveal all once they had Claire safely home and well away from the likes of her disreputable admirer.

Nita's resolve weakened, however, when faced with Claire's question and her bright, trusting eyes. "Well, you see, Sis…the truth is…" Nita took a deep breath.

"They are so beautiful, such an unusual mix. Where did you get them?"

"Claire, Fred and I didn't send them." She opened her purse, slid one hand inside and brought out the florist's card. "Here."

Claire took the card from Nita's outstretched hand. She hesitated before turning it over –staring at its blank backside. They must be from Mark. She had long since lost contact with her friends at school. Could they be from David? No, unless Nita had called him, David could not possibly know she was in the hospital.

The thought of David induced a wave of vertigo and Claire had to steady herself against the window ledge. She had felt the same unsteadiness when Nita had told her of David's remarriage. For all Claire knew, he and his new bride might soon be parents. She was not angry with David. She remembered how desperately he wanted a family. Still, his departure had left a gaping hole in Claire's heart, one she had tried to learn to live with, but whose presence she could never ignore.

Her hand trembling slightly, Claire flipped over the card and read its contents.

"Oh, my God." She had to steady herself again with her free hand. "He sent me flowers. First he saves my life −then he sends me flowers." Claire's breathing quickened.

Nita was alarmed by the wild look in her sister's eyes. "Calm down, sweetie. Come on, let's get you back to bed." But Claire would not move away from the window.

"Did he bring them, himself? Did you see him?" Claire grabbed onto Nita's arm, frantic for her reply.

"No, sweetie −he didn't bring them…But…" Nita seemed to have a sudden need to rearrange some of the flowers in the vase.

"But, what?" Nita was surprised by the strength of her sister's voice and knew there was no squirming out of the truth.

"He did come by to see you. I met him in the hall." Nita's tone became defensive. "But I didn't let him in. You were sleeping, you needed your rest."

Claire's eyes were glistening, looked almost feverish. Nita reflexively touched her forehead with the back of one hand.

"Nita, how could you send him away?" Claire stepped back from her sister. "He saved my life and that's how you thank him?"

"Claire, honey, listen to me." Nita grasped Claire's shoulders and shook her slightly. She waited for her sister's breathing to slow down. "I know you are grateful to this man. So am I. But we don't know anything about him. He looks like a street person. You know a lot of them have mental problems…"

"Unlike anyone you know!" Claire was still angry, but was not strong enough for a sustained fight with anyone much less her sturdy sister. She grabbed her IV pole and dragged it back to the bedside, sitting down heavily on the edge. Nita hesitantly followed.

"Nita," Claire did not want to risk driving her sister away again, nor behave in such a way as to insure another day in this room. "I know you're trying to protect me." She reached over and took her sister's hand. "But, I have a good feeling about this man, about the Duke. He's kind. I know he couldn't hurt anyone."

Nita studied her sister's eyes, once again clear and bright, showing no signs of the mania a moment before.

"You have to trust me," Claire continued, "though I know that's something I don't deserve."

"Don't deserve what?"

Claire and Nita both looked towards the door as Mark entered the room.

"Don't deserve what?" he repeated, walking towards the bed. Claire noted the concern in his eyes, his clean-shaven face appeared freshly scrubbed, as it always did no matter the time of day. She reached up and touched her hair.

"Oh, Mark, I'm so glad you're here. Wait until I tell you what's happened."

Mark was relieved to find his patient awake and, despite her disheveled appearance, looking rested and well. As he drew nearer, he detected something new in her face, not the dull apathy he had become accustomed to, nor the anger that had cut him so deeply during their last therapy session.

"What's happened, Claire? Tell me about it." Mark lapsed into counselor-mode as he drew the chair up to the bed and sat down. Nita tried to get his attention, waving her hand behind Claire's head. But Mark was completely focused on the woman in the bed.

"He was here, Mark. The Duke. He sent me flowers. Isn't it wonderful?" Claire pointed towards the window. It was then that Mark looked at Nita after glancing at the bouquet. She merely arched her eyebrows and rolled her eyes…a gesture Mark could not interpret.

"Mark. I have to find him…today. I have to thank him."

"Yes, I understand, Claire. But don't you think another night or two in the hospital would do you good? I'd like to start you on a new medication, with

Dr. Wright's approval. He may want to monitor you as it takes effect."

"No, Mark. No more drugs." Claire swallowed, trying to calm herself before continuing. She was well aware of the importance of appearing rational and in control, a skill learned years ago that had won her release from the other hospital.

"I feel fine…better than I have for a long time. You've got to believe me. I know what I'm doing. The Duke helped me and I need to thank him." Claire paused. "And I think, in some way, he needs my help."

Before Mark could respond, a nurse bustled into the room.

"Excuse me, folks. Dr. Wright wants me to discontinue your IV. Your blood work came back fine, young lady." She winked at Claire. "As soon as he gets the report from your therapist, you're free to go."

The pain as the nurse pulled out the needle made Claire nauseous, but the feeling soon passed as the nurse applied pressure to the wound. While waiting for the blood to clot, she gave Claire her discharge instructions. She was to go home with her sister and take it easy for a few days, be sure to eat a balanced diet and drink plenty of fluids.

"You do as the doctor says," she spoke over her shoulder after wrapping the IV line around the pole and rolling it noisily through the door.

Claire struggled to contain her elation at the prospect of being set free. "Mark, please, I want to go home. I'm fine –please believe me." Claire reached over and placed her hand on Mark's shoulder. "I have things to do…starting with a trip upstairs to the nursery."

"Nursery?" Mark looked at Nita.

"Claire wants to help me on the preemie ward –to rock the babies." Nita shook her head from side to side, hoping Claire would not notice and that Mark would get the message.

"I don't know, Claire. I'm not sure that's a good idea, at least not right now." Claire's eyes brimmed with tears but she tried hard to mask her desperation.

"Please, Mark. I need to do this. I need to start giving back…I've taken so much. It's important."

Mark's resolve weakened with each word. He still feared for his patient's health and sanity…for her safety. He also knew the hospital would not keep her unless he determined she was a risk to herself or to others. Claire had already been through so much. Maybe spending time with at-risk newborns would bring closure from the trauma of losing her own child. And Nita would be with her.

"O.K." Mark placed his hand on Claire's. "If you're sure you are strong enough. I'll go sign off on your chart. But, I want to see you in my office in two weeks. Promise?"

Claire reached over and hugged Mark so closely he could hardly breath. For most of his years in practice, he had stayed detached, had not become emotionally involved with his patients. But Claire touched something deep inside himself, something he could not even define.

He hugged her back. She was nothing but skin and bones, like a delicate flower that might wilt when touched. Still, he held her, burying his face in her wild hair.

"Um-um," Nita cleared her throat discreetly. Mark immediately released his grasp and pulled away, pushing Claire gently back towards the bed with both hands on her sharp shoulders, then stood up.

In his most dispassionate clinical voice, he spoke, "Well, then, I guess you're off." Claire looked up at him, her face suffused with the pink glow from the window. Was it love he saw in her eyes, or just gratitude? Mark turned, confused by the intensity of his own feelings. Had he stepped over the line into unprofessional behavior?

Mark paused at the doorway to wave good-bye, but Claire was already out of bed, pulling clothes from the drawer of her bedside table. Nita was right behind her, holding the back of her hospital gown together. She returned his wave along with a tentative smile.

As he walked towards the nurses' station, Mark said a silent prayer that he was doing the right thing. His brain told him she was nowhere near ready to be released into the world. But his heart still saw the new life in her eyes, still felt the pressure from their embrace, the quick beat of her heart against his chest.

"Maybe I'm the one who's losing control," he mumbled to himself, hoping no one would hear him and suggest that he needed to check himself into the hospital.

Chapter XVII

"I'm not an invalid, Nita. I can walk." Claire craned her neck to see her sister who was pushing the wheelchair down the corridor.

"Sorry, Sis, hospital regs. Until you're out the front door, they still consider you a patient." Nita patted Claire's shoulder. "Besides, it's a long way to the NICU. You might poop out and I doubt even I could carry you the whole way." Nita laughed nervously. She was still not convinced Claire was ready for this, but did not want to create a scene at the nurses' station where they had left Claire's overnight bag and the bouquet of flowers.

Claire had to close her eyes to quell the vertigo from the strobe-light effect of passing quickly under the bright fluorescent bulbs. The rush of cold antiseptic air felt refreshing after being cooped up in her warm tiny room. A rhythmic click from the wheels lulled her into a semi-slumber. She was aware of the change of air, heard the hum of the elevator as it lurched upwards, then stopped.

As Nita rolled the wheelchair onto the nursery floor, Claire opened her eyes. The hall lights were dim and she could just make out the words, "Restricted Access," on the door at the end of the corridor. Dim light also shone through the plate-glass-windows that covered the top half of the walls on either side. Through them, Claire could see nurses clad in surgical scrubs and masks, moving quickly about, occasionally stopping to check a monitor or switch off a blinking light.

Few sounds emitted from behind the closed entryway. Claire had expected to at least hear an infant cry. She found the silence almost eerie and shuddered as though a chill had passed through her body. Nita must have detected this subtle change, for she stopped halfway down the hall and came around to the front of the chair.

"Claire, are you sure you want to do this? Maybe we should come back when you've had time to rest." A line of worry bisected Nita's forehead. Claire reached over and traced it with her finger, as if to smooth it away. She did not want to cause her sister any more pain, but something strong and overpowering had compelled her to this place and she knew there was no turning back.

"No, Nita. I want to help –today. I need to. Please don't worry, I'll be O.K."

Nita stood a moment more, then glanced through the glass, catching the attention of a blue-clad nurse. "Wait here. I have to clear this with the charge nurse. I'll be right back."

Claire watched Nita as she stopped before entering the nursery to don a disposable gown and mask from a basket beside the door. Their heads nearly touching, Claire watched her sister converse with the nurse. At one point, Nita pointed towards the hall and the nurse turned towards Claire, paused, then waved before resuming the conversation.

They spoke for so long that Claire wondered if the nurse had found Nita's request a little risky, especially since, technically, Claire was still a patient…on top of the fact that she had no experience handling babies of any size.

Convinced the quest had been futile after all, Claire rose from the wheelchair, determined to see the tiny babies, even if she could not hold one. She walked over to the viewing glass and surveyed the inner room.

At first, she could see no babies at all. The space was dominated by large machines with various dials, buttons, and monitors, and an array of blinking lights. Transparent boxes lit by soft lights were nestled among the machines. Claire gasped when she first made out a still form inside an incubator, a tiny head turned towards the side, its body wrapped tightly in a pink blanket that looked no bigger than a moth's cocoon. The baby's arms were splayed to the side and her tiny chest rose and fell almost imperceptibly.

But what shocked Claire the most were the numbers of tubes and wires attached to the sleeping baby, lifelines hooking her precariousiy to the world. As she watched, the tiny face screwed up into a wrinkly mask, its mouth open in a perfect "o." But, even with her ear pressed to the glass, Claire could hear no sound or cry.

Claire was so engrossed in this scene, she did not realize Nita had left the room.

"Aren't they beautiful. 'Little Miracles,' I call them." Nita joined Claire, her face as proud as any grandmother.

Truthfully, Claire did not see the beauty in these impossibly small creatures with wrinkled skin and monkey-like faces. For the first time since announcing her intention to rock one of them, Claire wondered if she could really follow through. They looked so fragile, like beings from another planet that might dissolve if exposed to earth's atmosphere, much less to human touch.

"It took some talking to convince Mrs. Miller to let you help me, but I assured her you would do a good job." Nita turned to face Claire, "Are you ready?"

Claire looked again through the glass and took a deep breath before answering. "Yes, I'm ready," working hard to ignore the queasiness in her stomach.

"We can leave the wheelchair here. Come on." Claire followed Nita through another door into what appeared to be a scrub room. Nita motioned towards a large sink.

"First, you need to wash your hands and arms up to the elbow. Most of the babies have compromised immune systems and exposure to a bacteria or virus could be enough to kill them."

Nita's explanation did nothing to ease Claire's growing nervousness. "Oh, great," Claire thought, "someone else I can kill," though she tried to keep a blank expression as she followed Nita's lead, scrubbing her skin until it felt raw.

When the ablutions were finished, Nita helped Claire don a yellow disposable surgical gown and cap, mask, and, finally, latex gloves. Claire wondered if the babies knew there were human beings behind this scary costume.

Through the window of a door at the other end of the room, Claire could see an alcove furnished with two wooden rockers. It was into this space that Nita herded Claire next.

"Sit here, Sis. I want to give you some ground rules." Nita eased herself into one of the chairs, motioning Claire to the other.

"I know these babies look fragile, and in many ways, they are. But, they are amazingly resilient. Be sure to support their heads and backs. You want to hold them close to your body so they can feel your heat and hear your beating heart. They've proven that preemies who have been given maximum human contact actually thrive better than those kept exclusively in the incubator."

Claire tried to concentrate on Nita's authoritative voice, but her insides were quivering. She had tried so hard to forget her own baby, had avoided passing families in the park, or looking inside strollers. Holding a baby had been the last thing she wanted to do. And, yet, here she was, about to cradle someone else's child. What if she dropped it or hurt it in some way. Her breaths and heartbeat began to quicken.

Claire was just about to tell Nita that this had been a mistake, after all, when her sister disappeared inside the ward. Claire's head started to feel light.

"Breathe, Claire, breathe." She closed her eyes and sucked in the sterile, antiseptic air. "Breathe, Claire," she could hear David's voice. She tried to slow her breaths, but they became shallow. Her heart fluttered inside her chest. "Breathe, Claire."

"Hold your breath now and push." Claire knew she must take control of this irresistible force pulling her body apart. She took as deep a breath as possible, then pushed down, riding the top of the contraction, breathing, panting, breathing. She was in a tunnel. It was dark save for a tiny light at the end. Something pressed in on her, encircled her, smothered her.

"Breathe, Claire, now push," a voice reached her ears from some distant place. Claire was exhausted, but the weight pressing on her chest was suffocating her. She began to panic.

"I don't want to be here. Let me out." It was her own voice that she heard, or rather her voice as a child. She heard its plea over and over again, though no sound emitted from her parched lips. Then darkness closed in, became complete until even the tiny light at the end was snuffed.

"Help me." Claire pushed against the door with all of her strength, pushed and pushed. She could no longer breathe. There was no air. If she couldn't get it open, she would die.

With one last effort, Claire pushed until the door suddenly gave way. Bright lights flooded the space around her, so bright she could not open her eyes. But, the air was cool and she sucked it greedily into her aching lungs.

A baby started to cry, to wail. At first, the sound was far away, but started to come closer.

"My baby." Claire could not believe her ears. "My baby is crying." The sound was now so close she could hear the child's ragged gasp for air before emitting another cry.

Suddenly, Claire felt a weight on her belly. Was it Max? Was she at home? No, Max didn't cry. It's a baby, my baby. Our baby. Instinctively, she wrapped her arms around the now squirming form, so warm against her stomach.

"Oh, David," she opened her eyes and looked up, expecting to see her husband's face reflecting the same joy she was feeling.

"Claire, Claire, honey. Are you all right? Be careful, now. Remember to support the baby's head."

Claire recognized the voice and eyes above the surgical mask. But what was her sister doing in the delivery room? Where was David? He'd promised to stay with her until the baby was born.

"Claire!" Nita's voice was insistent, almost harsh. "Claire. You have to pay attention. I knew this would be too much for you. Here, let me take the baby."

"No!" Claire hugged the tiny body to her breast. Nita pulled back, worried the baby might be injured if her sister became agitated. She glanced quickly around to see if the nurses were watching, but they were all busy writing notes at their station and did not appear to notice.

"Claire, honey. Are you all right?"

Nita knelt down in front of her sister's chair, wedging the weight of her body against Claire's knees, poised to catch the infant if she fell. Claire opened her eyes, puzzled by the dim light. She glanced around the room, at the other rocking chair before realizing she, herself, was sitting upright, not spread-eagled on the delivery table. Had it been a dream or hallucination? The cry had been so real. But, how could it be? Her baby was dead.

Tears rolled down Claire's cheeks. They splashed onto the face of the baby that was still nestled in her arms, engendering a new wail of protest.

Claire looked down at the source of this anguish, into a red perfect face, its tiny nose and eyes drawn tightly together, its mouth open. A doll-like hand wormed its way free from the tight blanket. The fingers opened and closed as if desperate to find something on which to cling. Claire put out her gloved finger and the hand curled tightly around it.

"Oh, please don't cry, little one." Claire rocked the child gently back and forth in her arms. "Hush, now, it's O.K. Mommy's here. Don't cry."

Nita managed to maintain her position, despite the chair's movement. She tried not to panic, struggling to find a strategy to wrest the child from her sister's arms without provoking some violent response. She debated calling for help, but was afraid she'd lose her own right to rock the babies if anyone realized what was happening.

As Claire studied the infant's face, her breathing began to slow, as did her heart. She began to croon softly through the mask. Slowly, the room around her came into focus, her sister still kneeling at her feet, the soft beep of the monitors in the next room, which she could just hear over the baby's cry. Slowly, she came back to the present, to the reality of her life —alone and childless.

Claire continued to rock gently, singing softly to the infant until the room became quiet and the child closed her eyes.

Nita could see this process take place in her sister. Convinced the baby was in no danger, she struggled to her feet, her hips and knees stiff and aching.

"Claire, I want you to meet Rebecca. She was born four weeks ago, two months early, so small she could fit in my hand. I've been coming to rock her to give her mother a break so she can spend some time at home with her other children." Nita pulled a small bottle from the pocket of her gown and gave it to Claire. Its warmth felt comforting against her hand. "At first, she had to be tube-fed. The therapists worked with her until she learned to suck. I think she's hungry. Do you want to feed her?"

Claire made no move to bring the nipple to the baby's mouth. "Rebecca, what a pretty name." Nita decided not to hurry her sister, realizing something deep and powerful was happening, something necessary to her sister's recovery.

"Hello, little Rebecca." Claire spoke softly, but the baby heard and opened her eyes and appeared to try to focus on Claire's face. Blue rims encircled her large, dark pupils.

Rebecca squirmed again in Claire's arms and opened her mouth to register another protest. It was then that Claire became aware of the bottle that she tipped upright, placing the nipple against the baby's lips. Rebecca moved her head from side to side, frantically searching for the nipple and when found, clamped her lips around it and began to suck noisily.

"She's hungry." Claire looked up at Nita with a look of satisfaction. Her smile did much to relieve Nita's anxiety as to just how this scene would play out.

"Oh, she's an eater alright. The pediatrician told me last week that when she gains 8 more ounces, he's going to let her go home. I have no doubt she'll meet that goal soon."

Claire looked back down at her ward, at the tiny hand still clutching her finger. She marveled at the detail of each perfect digit, the intricate network of veins and capillaries visible beneath the thin luminous skin…so like her daughter's hand before the doctor ripped her away.

Claire crooned softly as the baby sucked. Nita started breathing normally as she watched her sister slowly return, as her face became transformed with a mother's tenderness.

"Nita?" Claire looked up. "Do you think Rebecca and I could be alone for a moment?"

"I'm not sure that's a good idea, Sis. You don't seem to be quite yourself." Nita hoped her words would not evoke any agitation in her sister who continued to calmly rock the feeding baby.

"Please, Nita. I need some time with her –alone. I won't let anything happen to her…I promise."

Nita could never resist those pleading eyes and, against her better judgement, started walking towards the door. "I'll be right outside if you need me."

"We'll be fine," Claire watched until her sister closed the door behind her, then assumed her position on the other side of the glass.

For a few minutes, Claire concentrated on the child as she drained the two-ounce bottle. Then, instinctively, Claire brought the child up to her shoulder, careful to support her head and neck as she gently patted the tiny back. A few moments later, a loud belch broke the silence and Claire laughed as she brought the baby back down to rest in her arms.

"That wasn't very ladylike," she chided.

Rebecca lay peacefully in Claire's arms, her eyes now wide and open, the pupils wandering a bit before focusing on Claire's face. Claire looked deeply in the baby's eyes before speaking.

"Rebecca, do you mind if I borrow your name?" The baby flailed her free hand in response, pursing her lips as though in thought.

"You see, I had a baby girl just like you. She was perfect, too –except for a tiny hole in her heart, so small no one knew it was there –until she was born. I didn't get a chance to talk to her, to tell her how much she was loved—to tell her she was the most important thing that ever happened to me." Claire paused for breath as a fresh tear fell onto the baby's cheek. She blinked her eyes and let out a squeak.

"I never got a chance to name her –but I would like to now, with your permission, of course." Another squeak.

"Rebecca, if you can hear me, I just want you to know that your Daddy and I love you so much. I'm sorry I wasn't strong enough to keep you on this earth...but I will be strong, now –for you...Sweet Rebecca." The tears became a flood of sorrow and grief, of disappointment and anger, and, finally, of deep, true joy, a joy Claire had never experienced before, as she sat and rocked this tiny miracle.

"You have a good life now, little one. Thank you."

Nita had entered the room when Claire began crying, waited until her sobs abated before suggesting gently that it was time for baby Rebecca to take a nap.

Claire released her hold, but not reluctantly. She realized she was ready to let her go -this Rebecca -this living link to her own dear child.

Nita left with the baby then returned to the room where Claire still sat rocking.

"I'm ready to go home now."

"I know," Nita placed a supportive hand under Claire's elbow and helped her to stand, but once upright, Claire brushed her arm away, stood tall and straight before walking into the scrub room and discarding her protective gear.

"Madame, your chariot awaits." Nita rolled the wheelchair to the door. Claire bowed before sitting down and settling herself as regally as a queen on her throne.

The nurses in the ward raised their heads to find the source of the raucous laughter coming from the hall just as the elevator door closed on what appeared to be two very happy women.

Chapter XVIII

Claire and Nita were still laughing when they reached the nurses' station to pick up Claire's belongings. The nurse standing behind the counter looked up crossly and put her finger to her lips to shush the unruly pair, barely recognizing her former patient. As they drew closer, she was delighted at Claire's transformation and could not help but join in the fun.

"Hush, you ruffians," she directed towards Claire and Nita in a loud whisper. "There're sick people on this floor, you know. We can't have any laughter. It might be contagious."

The nurse's words triggered a new round of uncontrollable giggling which Nita and Claire tried unsuccessfully to suppress.

"Now pick up your bag and begone, young lady. And I never want to see you again, at least not here." Claire recognized the same nurse that had taken out her IV.

"On my honor, I will try to do my duty, to God and my country..." Claire brought three fingers up to her forehead in her best Girl Scout salute, but giggles

168

once again got the best of her. She wiped away the tears streaming down her face as the nurse rounded the counter and delivered a firm, maternal hug to her patient.

"You take good care of yourself —and your big sister."

Nita beamed from her post behind the chair.

"Here's your bag," the nurse continued. "And don't forget your beautiful flowers. Oh, and I almost forgot, you have a visitor waiting in the lounge down the hall." She caught the look of disapproval on Nita's face. "I hope that was alright," she hastily added.

"A visitor?" Claire wondered if Mark had returned, but surely the nurse would know who he was.

"Claire, you've had enough for one day. I'm sure whoever it is will understand you need to rest." Nita balanced the flower arrangement in one hand and attempted to push the chair towards the elevator. But, Claire stood up quickly nearly falling over as the chair hit the back of her knees.

"Nita, please. That would be rude. Let me at least see who it is," Claire pleaded.

Despite the positive ending to the session in the nursery, Nita was still wary of Claire's ability to handle another emotional situation and she was certain of the identity of the visitor.

"O.K. Sit down. You're still a patient, remember? I'll give you five minutes to talk to whoever it is —five minutes!"

As Nita awkwardly pushed the chair down the hall and through the door of the lounge, her worst fears were realized. There on the couch opposite was the man who called himself "the Duke." Protectively, she pulled backwards on the chair just as Claire rose. The sudden lightness threw Nita off guard and she had to let go of the wheelchair handle to keep from spilling the flowers. Recovering her balance and with righteous strength, she took two large steps, planting herself as a shield between Claire and the stranger.

"Nita, what are you doing?" Claire managed, despite her shaky legs, to walk around her sister. The Duke was already on his feet. With a flourish of one hand, he bowed deeply.

"Good afternoon, m'lady Claire. How nice it is to see you in an upright position."

Nita sniffed disapprovingly at this somewhat suggestive greeting. Claire stood still, her hand to her open mouth, her eyes as round as if she had seen a ghost. This man's face had been in her mind, in her dreams, for days. Sometimes she had doubted his existence, but remembered the sickening sound of his body hitting the pavement and knew that had been real, no matter if the rest of the fantasy was just that.

"It was so kind of you to come, Duke…er…Daniel," Nita stammered, "but, as you can see, my sister is tired and in no shape for a visit. Now, if you'll excuse us…" Nita attempted to grab Claire's elbow, but her sister had already moved with surprising quickness over to the sofa where she sat down, patting the seat beside her.

"Please, Duke, sit down. My sister has forgotten her manners," she said sweetly as she glared at Nita.

Their eyes locked for a moment. Claire could feel her heart beating wildly against her ribs, but managed to keep the same expression and not look away.

Finally, Nita broke the stare and sighed in defeat. "Five minutes, remember, and I'll be right outside the door." After "shooting daggers" at the Duke, Nita rolled the chair just outside, pushed it up against the wall and sat down, with an ear close to the open door.

"Please, sit down." Claire patted the sofa again, before reaching back to retie the ponytail Nita had hastily knotted before they left for the nursery.

"M'lady mustn't fret. She could not make herself more beautiful."

Claire could feel the blood rushing to her cheeks and looked away as the Duke settled himself on the sofa beside her. She did not know what to say or how to respond to his compliment. Instead, she focused on his worn shoes and frayed pant cuffs. He was wearing the same dirty shirt and vest underneath the long overcoat as the day they had first met in front of the diner.

Summoning the courage to look at his face, Claire concentrated first on his chin, or rather the inch-long stubble that reached up on either side to his ears. Her eyes jumped up to his greasy hair, matted at the crown and hanging in unruly ringlets to his shoulders. Maybe Nita was right, maybe he was just a bum, maybe he was dangerous. But, then she saw his eyes, clear and alert, intelligent and gentle, remembered the kind way he had helped her to get home, the way his hands had kept her from falling down the stairs, the way he had saved her from choking. She thought of those beautiful flowers that had been sent by someone she had tried to kill...and knew she was in no danger in the company of such a man.

"I want..."

"You see..."

They both began speaking at once, then stopped. After an awkward silence, the Duke motioned Claire to go ahead.

"I just wanted to thank you...for...for everything you've done for me in the past week. You don't even know me, and yet..."

The Duke brought a finger to her lips without touching them. "Let me introduce myself," the Duke began in his aristocratic accent, then, he paused a moment before continuing, this time in a nasally Yankee twang. "My name is Daniel, Daniel Redding. And you, I understand, are Claire –lovely Claire."

"Yes, Claire McKinney –you're not English?" Claire did not wait for an answer before continuing. "You must hate me. Did I hurt you –is your head O.K.? Oh, I feel just terrible." Claire's voice cracked. Daniel grabbed her hand to calm her. She remembered that grip, the large, lined hands. With their touch she could feel her muscles relax, as if the tension were rolling down her arms and legs and disappearing into the floral-patterned sofa.

"You didn't hurt me, really –just knocked the breath out of me. The last thing I remember is an angel bending over me. But, I knew she was just a dream, for the next time I opened my eyes, she was gone."

"Oh, I went inside to get help and when I came back out you had disappeared. I thought I'd killed you and someone had already hauled you away —or, worse, that I had imagined the whole thing—that you really did not exist at all." Claire became flustered, "Of course, it would have been far worse for you if you were actually dead…" Claire lifted her head and looked into Daniel's face.

"I haven't been well."

"I know. I knew you were in trouble that first day. I thought I might be able to help…that's why I came to your apartment. I hadn't expected such a violent reception."

Claire looked down at her lap and slowly pulled her hand away, shame and guilt at not having trusted him bringing tears to her eyes.

"And then I saw you again, at the diner. I didn't know whether to put up my "dukes" or run like hell the other way." Daniel held his fists up in front of his face like a prizefighter and smiled. "But, I've always been a sucker for a pretty face."

Before Claire could react, Nita stomped into the room. "O.K., time's up. Let's go, Sis."

Claire was not ready to go. She could not simply walk away from someone who within a few brief meetings had managed to connect with her on such a deep level. She owed him more than five minutes.

"Nita, I'm fine. Daniel and I have some things to discuss. Please." Claire spoke firmly to her sister who was standing as usual with her legs apart and hands planted on her hips.

Despite her resolve to protect Claire, she did not wish to upset her sister and was secretly pleased at this new act of defiance. What possible harm could come to her in this small room with Nita standing sentry, even if it was in the company of this disreputable figure? She also knew that spending time with him was the only way to break down Claire's obsession with the man. Surely, another five minutes in close proximity to his body odor would be enough for any one.

"O.K., but I'll be right outside." Nita threw Daniel another look before exiting. Claire waited until she could hear her settle into the wheelchair before continuing.

"The flowers are beautiful. It was so kind of you to send them –but everything you've done for me has been kind. Why? Why would you help a perfect stranger…especially me?" Claire felt emboldened by her victory over Nita and compelled to know more about this man's motives.

"I saw something in your eyes that first day – something lost and hurt –a pain so intense I could feel it myself." A tear slid down Claire's cheek which Daniel wiped away with one finger. "I wanted to help in some way." He looked directly in her eyes. "It's what I do."

"But, why?" Claire still was unable to understand someone motivated only by kindness, asking nothing in return. She had read about such love as a kid in Sunday School but had never experienced it in what she considered the real world of adults. A picture of Jesus, one that had been on a colored plate in her Bible, flashed in her mind –the same hair, the same smile, the same kind eyes…That was it! That explained everything. She was sitting in the presence of Jesus Christ, himself.

Claire burst out in sudden laughter, as uncontrollable as the bout earlier in the hall. Daniel became alarmed as her voice took on the wild sound of hysteria. He was just about to go out into the hall and get help from Nita, when Claire managed to calm herself.

Wiping her eyes, she put her hand on Daniel's arm, this time forcing him to look at her directly. "Please Duke, I mean Daniel. Why do you help people like me?"

"A penance, I guess…" his voice and gaze trailed off before he shook himself, sat up straighter and sent Claire a courtly smile. "If my lady will excuse me, I need to speak to yon knight guarding the gate." He rose and bowed before crossing gracefully to the door and peering out towards the wheelchair. Nita's eyes were shut, her chin resting on her bosom. A slight rattle escaped through her lips with each breath.

Claire watched his movements anxiously, terrified she had scared him off before learning more about her own strange "knight." She held her breath until he once again settled himself beside her.

"Now, enough about me." Daniel again dropped the pretentious accent, spoke in what he hoped was an encouraging and non-threatening tone, the tone of a therapist Claire later thought.

"If I know where this pain is coming from, perhaps I can help. Do you feel like sharing with the "Old Duke?"

Claire laughed. His clothes were worn and tattered, his beard and hair were speckled with gray, but the skin around his eyes looked soft and smooth. "Old," she reasoned, must be the way he felt. She could certainly relate.

Something about Daniel made her feel safe and at ease, as if he were asking to take on her burden, no matter how heavy. Claire did not feel the same defensiveness that had kept her from being completely truthful about her feelings with Mark, or all the others before him.

"Are you sure about this?"

"Yes." Daniel leaned back into the sofa, brought one long leg up to rest casually on the other and waited patiently for Claire to speak.

She started from the beginning, or as far back as she could remember. She spoke of her parents' unhappy marriage and her eating disorder. She even told him of the night her father had locked her in the closet, remembering for the first time each terrifying detail. She described her first hospitalization and the way she had tricked the doctor in order to be released. Her voice, at first shaky, became stronger as she spoke of her determination to save her parents' marriage and the guilt and devastation she had felt when her father had left them.

Claire barely touched the happy years at college, the job she loved, and the first years of her marriage to David. The Duke watched Claire's face intently, nodding his head, speaking an occasional word of encouragement. He let Claire talk on and on, did not even notice the changing light as the afternoon turned into evening, the occasional nurse's head that appeared inquiringly at the door.

Claire was amazed that she could recount the details of their baby's death and David's departure without breaking down...was it because of Daniel's obvious concern or had something happened upstairs in the nursery? She would think about that later, for she noticed as her sad story wound down, Daniel had closed his eyes. Claire knew she had talked too much, that of course he had become bored and fallen asleep.

Daniel was so still, for a moment Claire panicked, stood to try and walk to the hall, but her legs would not hold her weight and she fell back onto the seat. He still did not move and afraid, once more, that she had killed him, this time with too many words and too much emotion, she reached up to touch his face, merely brushing the whiskers. Without opening his eyes, he spoke softly.

"I'm not asleep, Claire. I was just thinking about your story. We're a lot alike, you know."

Claire was relieved to find him still breathing, but try as she may, she could not think how they were alike –in any way. Here was a man who lived for others. Most of her life, she had dwelled upon her own happiness or sorrow, her own hurt and heartbreak. Why did he think they could possibly be alike?

"What do you mean?"

"I lost a child, too..." The Duke looked away, his eyes glistening. "Or rather, he lost me."

For a moment, Claire feared he might break down, but he turned his face back towards her, one tear absorbed by his beard. Claire knew it was her turn to be the therapist, to at least attempt to focus on someone else's problems for a change.

"Tell me about it, if you want to." She settled herself into the couch, tried to assume the same body language he had used an hour before. Neither one of them noticed the nurse tiptoe in and turn on the table lamp. Claire was only aware of a soft glow on the side of his face that made him look almost beatific.

Daniel swiped at his face with a dirty coat sleeve and seemed reluctant to continue.

"Come on, it's only fair. You know all about me. Now it's your turn to spill your guts." Claire glanced towards the door. "I've got all night."

"There's not much to tell, really. I had it all once –a Ph.D., a tenured position at a prestigious college, a marriage to one of my promising graduate students." Daniel shook his head. "Before my wife finished her degree, she became pregnant. It was all she could think about –becoming a mother. With each month she became more and more distracted, dropped her classes. I did little to stop her. I was delighted, too, at the thought of becoming a father. Then, I would have it all, you see." Daniel took a deep breath. "I was on top of the world."

Claire knew this story did not have a happy ending and steeled herself for the next installment. Her back, arms, and legs ached, but she felt this dialogue, this moment was a watershed of sorts and ignored the physical discomfort. She covered Daniel's hand with her own and gave it a gentle squeeze. His eyes were unfocused or rather focused on something she couldn't see.

"Please, Daniel, go on."

Her voice brought him back to the present. After taking another deep breath, he continued. "The baby was perfect when he was born –8 pounds. He came into the world squealing and kicking. A son…my son…my perfect son." Again, his eyes focused on something distant.

"The first years were wonderful. My wife decided to postpone finishing her degree until our son -we named him Thomas -went to school. It was fine by me. I had it all –perfect job, beautiful wife, strapping son…" His voice quavered.

"Is this too hard, Daniel? We can stop if you want." Claire tried to give him an out.

"No. I've kept this bottled up for too long…" It was Daniel's face that became flushed, his feverish eyes glistening. Claire settled back into the sofa.

"When Thomas was three, we started noticing little things. He began falling, staggering when he walked. Simple things he had been able to do, like holding a crayon or putting together Lego's, were suddenly hard. At first we just thought he was going through a growth spurt, regressing a little. But, one day he fell and just lay there until we picked him up. We took him to a specialist, a neurologist. They poked him with needles, did a score of tests. And, then, we got the diagnosis." Daniel stopped and Claire gave his hand another encouraging squeeze.

"Thomas has Duchenne's -one of the most devastating kinds of muscular dystrophy. Over the next few months we learned all we could about the disease. There is no cure. The researchers were just beginning to explore gene replacement therapy...but it's still experimental. The doctors told us our beautiful son would slowly lose the strength in his arm and leg muscles. They told us that he would eventually need a wheelchair, probably by the age of ten...and then it would affect the muscles of his lungs and heart and he would more than likely die of respiratory failure before the age of twenty." Daniel swallowed. The last part of his narrative seemed hardest to deliver.

"My life ended, then...my perfect wonderful life. At first, my wife and I faced this new challenge with typical intellectual zeal. Thomas may not have a long life, but, by God, he would have a good one..."

"But, one day, as I watched him playing with some other children, not being able to keep up with them on the playground, it suddenly came crashing down on me. I would lose my son...I felt myself falling into despair, and, like Thomas, could not pull myself up."

"My wife and I argued incessantly. I began spending nights at the office coming home only to change my clothes. We stopped speaking and I started waiting until I knew Thomas was asleep to enter our house. Things got worse. I slept through my classes, missed departmental meetings. Rumors began to circulate around campus that I was having an affair with a student -though that, at least, wasn't true. The Dean sent memo's that I did not answer until one day he called and asked me to come to his office. He was nice enough, suggested maybe I needed a sabbatical."

"It didn't help that I blew up at him —told him he could take his sabbatical and put it you-know-where. He must have thought I'd gone mad —and, perhaps, I had."

"All I knew was that life, at least my life, didn't make sense anymore and I knew I could not bear to watch my son deteriorate and die. He and his mother would be better off without me."

Daniel closed his eyes, again and breathed deeply several times.

"And so, I left them —my wife and son, the college, my career. I faded away…hoping to die before Thomas did." Daniel looked at Claire, "I called a friend a month or so ago. He told me my wife finished her degree and is teaching at the same college. Thomas is in fourth grade and is apparently very bright…at least he inherited one good trait."

Claire realized it was important to stay still until he finished. Daniel looked down for a long time and did not move, but Claire knew better than to touch him.

"So, you see, Claire, we are a lot alike —you and me. We both ran away from our problems, just in different ways." Daniel reached over and placed his hand on Claire's cheek.

"But there is a difference…" Claire brought her hand up to cover his and looked deeply into his troubled blue eyes.

"Your child is still alive…"

Chapter XIX

"Mark, I need to know why I hurt people who try to help me." Claire was back in her therapist's office, two weeks to the day since her release from the hospital.

"If you could have seen his face –I hurt him, Mark –this kind man." Claire sat on the edge of her chair, leaning forward, her face bright, her hands dancing as she recounted the events of that night, of her encounter with the Duke.

Mark could not believe the change in his client. There was no trace of the pitiful woman he had visited two weeks before. The abrupt change made him feel uncomfortable, as though their roles were reversed and she was the one in complete control of the session.

"Claire, I don't…"

"I didn't mean to, Mark. I was just trying to help him…like he helped me." Claire paused, closed her eyes and took a deep breath. She could still see Daniel's face, the pain in his eyes, his opened mouth poised to speak before he stood abruptly and rushed from the room.

"I might as well have pushed him off the steps again." Claire shuddered and shook her head. Her long, curly hair swept around her face. Mark realized he had never seen her wear it down. He liked the way it framed her face accentuating the darkness of her large eyes. Why hadn't he noticed the loveliness of those eyes?

"Mark!" Claire was irritated by this lapse of attention, interpreting it as Mark's disinterest in her story. A few weeks before, she would have been hurt by such behavior.

"Mark, are you listening to me?" Claire stamped her foot, hoping the sound would bring him out of this stupor.

Mark visibly jumped. Redness crept up his neck into his face, sweat beads popped out on his forehead. He shifted uneasily in his chair.

"Claire," Mark could not bring himself to look again directly at his client. "I don't...I'm sorry. Please go on." When she did not respond, he forced himself to look in her direction and nodded his head.

"I just wanted him to see that he still had a chance to connect with his child –a chance I never got..." Claire's eyes filled with tears as her voice quavered. Mark struggled to appear sympathetic, but he could focus on little else than those eyes, the way the moisture caught the light and made them sparkle.

"He must have thought I was criticizing him for leaving his family, for running away." Claire reached up and brushed a tear from her cheek then placed the same hand on Mark's knee.

"But, I didn't mean it that way. Who am I to judge anyone? He was right —I ran away, too. It wasn't just David. I see that now." She leaned back in her chair and gazed up at the ceiling as if her last few sentences were a revelation she needed time to ponder.

Mark waited for Claire to continue. But the room was silent, save for the pounding of a distant jackhammer on the street below.

"Claire, I…" Mark swallowed. "I can't continue seeing you."

Claire did not respond immediately, still lost in her last thoughts. A slight time elapsed before his words registered and, when they did, she sat up straight and cocked her head.

"What did you say?"

Mark looked down again knowing he could not speak the necessary words while looking into those eyes.

"I've stepped over the line, Claire." His tone was flat.

"What line? What are you talking about?" Claire began to panic. For months now, Mark had been her anchor, her only hold to sanity. She knew she was stronger but not strong enough yet to be cut adrift.

"I mean," Mark labored to control his own growing emotion. "I can no longer be objective where you're concerned. I care about you too much." He forced himself to look at her face, her eyes now wild and confused.

"What do you mean, you care about me too much? Isn't that part of your job?"

"Claire...you don't understand. My feelings for you..." Mark swallowed and fidgeted with the pen he held in his hand before continuing. "I think I'm..." He looked up, then, blinking his eyes furiously, partly to keep back the tears that he did not want Claire to see, but also to keep her face out of focus, making the next few words easier to speak.

"You're not just my patient anymore. I..."

"Mark, wait!" Claire blurted out suddenly before he could finish the sentence. Her head swam and she had to grip the armrests of her chair to keep herself from falling.

"Mark...I don't know what to say." And, in truth, she didn't. How many times over the past few months had she fantasized about this moment, about the prospect of a life linked to this man...the man who had saved her from herself? But, something had happened to her in the past weeks. She was not the same needy woman who had clung so desperately to her therapist. She had begun to feel whole and healed, to see herself as a strong, capable person...and it felt so good. Now, Mark's near-profession of love was like a slap knocking her off balance, threatening to destroy this new welcome sense of herself.

Before saying anything else, she looked across at the brown curls that touched his strong jaw line, marveling at the fact that they summoned no feelings of yearning, just an overwhelming sense of gratitude.

"Mark," she said softly, trying to choose words that would inflict no added pain, "I think I'm the one who stepped over the line. I didn't mean to give you the wrong impression…or to hurt you." She stopped, aware that she was now in charge of the session. She wanted to touch him, to comfort him the way he had comforted her again and again.

"You have helped me so much…" Seeing the hope drain from his brown eyes, she reached over and took his hand. It felt limp and lifeless.

"I'm strong, now –I'm not the same person that first crawled into your office with scarcely enough strength or will to keep breathing." Claire let go of his hand and touched his chin, lifting his face gently, forcing him to look into her eyes.

"You've done too good a job, Doctor. Your patient is healed." She smiled then leaned over and kissed Mark's sweaty forehead. "I will always be grateful."

Claire rose and walked to the door, then turned towards her former therapist who was still staring at her empty chair. "Thank you for caring."

Mark sat perfectly still until the last echo of her footsteps in the hallway melted into the perfect silence of the room. He could hear his heart beating in his chest, could feel the ache where a piece was missing, and chuckled softly at the irony of his situation.

"You're right, Claire." He rose from his desk and stood by the window, looking down at the street until his client emerged through the building's door. He watched as she crossed the street with her head held high, her long hair swaying back and forth across her straight shoulders. He continued watching as she walked confidently down the sidewalk, disappeared around the corner and was gone from his sight and from his life.

His own shoulders drooping slightly, Mark returned to his desk and collapsed onto his chair. Struggling to concentrate, he forced himself to relive the session with Claire –to recall every word they had spoken to each other.

It had not gone as planned. He had merely intended to suggest to his client that, as far as he was concerned, he had failed to help her, had failed to keep her safe from harm, and, that to continue to grow and heal, she would need to meet with someone else.

But, he could also see how she might have misinterpreted his carefully chosen words as some adolescent admission of love.

Minutes passed as Mark sat lost in this reverie. He knew he did not love Claire, not as a man loves a woman. But, still, she had touched something deep in his soul, something that was still vibrating to the rhythm of that maddening jackhammer that had resumed its beat. She had touched something that had gotten in the way of the therapeutic process his professor had carefully outlined on the cold classroom blackboard only a few years before.

Mark sighed deeply before checking his watch, realizing he needed to prepare for his next session. As he reached across to close the manila folder resting on the desktop, a tear rolled off his cheek and onto the last page of notes. Not noticing, he opened the drawer marked "Discharged" and inserted Claire's case file.

Mark would not see the blot of ink left by that errant tear until years later when he was researching material for a presentation. But it would only remind him of a time when he had been young and indiscreet...and only vaguely of eyes as deep and dark as the stain.

Chapter XX

The sun was so bright when Claire stepped out onto the sidewalk, that she was forced to pause a moment and retrieve her sunglasses from her purse. Once her eyes had adjusted, she marveled at the bright clear air so rare on warm days in the city. Her ears filled with the surrounding sounds of passing cars and trucks, sidewalk conversations, and the distant rhythmic thud of the jack hammer, the latter setting the beat for her feet that seemed to move without her conscious will.

As she walked past the group of commuters waiting at the bus stop, she was aware only of the graceful way her body moved, of the way, once freed from thought, her brain directed each muscle to contract and relax in perfect timing. It was as if something magical were propelling her forward. Her limbs felt light, her lungs sucked in the morning air, delivering just the right amount of oxygen to each cell. Her heart, too, was beating at just the right rate to sustain the fluid motion.

Claire walked for blocks contemplating the miracle of her own earthly body, how well it worked when unencumbered by the weight of negative thoughts and doubts, of decisions and regrets. This must be how it feels to walk on the moon, she mused, without the drag of gravity…to know the slightest effort could free one from the surface to bounce off and touch the stars.

When finally convinced there was no need to direct her body, that it worked perfectly on its own, Claire let her mind fill again with memories of the events of the past two weeks. Two weeks? Was that all that separated this new self from the hollow husk she had been before?

Just the thought of that old self made her cringe. If Mark had professed his love to that Claire, she would have fallen at his feet and begged to be lifted up, begged to ride behind him on his white steed as they rode off into the sunset.

The image that appeared in her mind was so comical, Claire stopped abruptly in the middle of a block, looked up to the sky and let out a loud whoop of laughter. Several passersby gave her a wide berth and sidelong glances. But, Claire was completely unaware of the attention her behavior engendered, nor did she notice the looks of appreciation thrown her way by several men, once she resumed her jaunty march. One of them even hung up his cell phone to watch her pass, mesmerized by the swing of her hips and the wide smile that lit her face.

"I feel like a new person," Claire spoke beneath her breath. But wasn't that what Nita had said a few days before when she stopped at the apartment to check up on her sister?

Nita could not believe the change in Claire since coming home from the hospital. She had convinced Claire to spend at least a week with her and Fred while they took turns coaxing her to rest and eat.

But, after only a few days, Claire pronounced herself well enough to return to her own apartment and to Max who met his master with a look of disgust. As soon as Claire sat down, however, her cat wasted no time before jumping up and settling himself on her lap for what he hoped would be a long, uninterrupted nap. Claire welcomed the weight of his warm, silky body and the familiar embrace of the soft pillows. She closed her eyes and slept deeply for hours without even one unpleasant dream.

When they both woke the next morning, Claire attacked the kitchen, scrubbing the counters and floors, cleaning the refrigerator and ridding the room of the odor of spoiled milk and cat food.

That afternoon, Claire took the money Nita and Fred had forced on her to Dulaney's Market, where she filled the grocery cart with cheese, eggs, vegetables and fruit, and, of course, cat food. On her way to the register she grabbed a baggette of French bread sticking out of a bin.

"So, I see you've decided to eat," Mrs. Dulaney remarked as she checked Claire's groceries. "Wait a minute." Claire stood at the counter as the woman disappeared. Through the front window she watched the redheaded boy sweep the front walk, stopping occasionally to rearrange the oranges or polish an apple. Once, he looked up and threw a teenage smirk in Claire's direction. She replied with a cheery "Hi" and was pleased when he looked down to hide his blushing face.

"Here," Mrs. Dulaney returned to her post, handing Claire a parcel wrapped in white butcher paper. "Put a little meat on those bones and you just might get a man, yet!"

"How much do I owe you for it?" Claire called to her departing back, the older woman did not seem to hear.

"Thanks, Mrs. Dulaney," she called a little louder as she placed the mysterious package in the top of her grocery bag and walked out the door past the embarrassed boy who could not help but follow Claire with his eyes as she walked quickly away.

Once back in her apartment, Claire unwrapped the white paper to reveal several thick slabs of smoky smelling bacon. The aroma caused her stomach to contract, reminding her she had forgotten to eat lunch.

"What do you think of that, Max? Old lady Dulaney's all right, after all." Claire hurried to pull out her mother's heavy cast iron skillet, placing it on the front burner of the stove. When she felt the heat rising from its surface, she laid the strips one at a time, crosswise in the pan. The pops and crackles along with the pungent smell that quickly permeated the small kitchen's air reminded her of mornings when she was young.

Claire closed her eyes and could still see her mother's back as she stood before the stove. Her movements were as deft and graceful as a symphony conductor —turning the bacon with one hand, cracking eggs with the other, pushing slices of bread down into the toaster —all to the accompaniment of her favorite songs.

How happy her mother had seemed even so early in the day, that is, until her husband shut her up with some criticism or comment. Claire remembered the sudden silence in the room save for the frying bacon and the crinkling of her father's newspaper. She had not thought of her father for days and the image of his sour face brought the bitter taste of bile to her mouth and for a moment she thought she might wretch onto the bacon and grease.

Claire had no idea where her father was now. For all she knew, he was dead. Except for an occasional birthday card postmarked from another city, Claire had not heard from him since he fulfilled his final obligation, paying the tuition for her senior year in college. He had not even come to watch his daughter graduate. Wherever he was, Claire hoped he was alone, that his second wife had had the sense and strength her mother had lacked to leave him before he ruined her life as well. Maybe he no longer had a home, was forced to beg on the streets, living hand to mouth, relying on the kindness of strangers...It would serve him right!

The kindness of strangers. The image of her father's face beneath a day's old beard, his starched shirts wrinkled and stained, his neatly creased slacks frayed, was so ridiculous she began to laugh until the mental picture abruptly changed. The features sharpened, the eyes turned a deep shade of blue…

The odor of scorched bacon brought Claire's attention back to the stove. She grabbed a dishtowel and wrapped it around the skillet handle, shoving the heavy pan to the back burner. She looked down, in horror, at the curled twists of black carbon swimming in their bath of grease and sighed in defeat. Suddenly tired, she abandoned any thoughts of eating that night and walked back to her bed, her appetite ruined by the smell and the unpleasant thoughts.

Claire held her head in her hands to steady her now spinning brain. Max jumped into her lap and she began stroking his fur, hoping the repetitive motion would calm her racing heart and rid her mind of its images. The first image was that of her father's face, then the Duke's face, then both faces blended into one —a composite of their best and worst features —showing kindness, then cruelty, then kindness. She remembered the despair that she had seen on Daniel's face -his open mouth, the hurt in his blue eyes, the final look he had given Claire that night in the hospital.

Claire hugged Max so tightly, trying to dispel her growing panic, that he wriggled out of her arms to keep from being smothered.

"How could I have been so cruel?" She spoke out loud to Max, then the apartment walls. "He was so kind to me." A fresh wave of remorse forced tears from her eyes and they slid uncontrollably down her cheeks.

"But, he left his family, Max. He walked out on them. Just like my own father, Max..." She directed her words towards the windowsill where Max had retreated. "He was so kind to me. How could the same person be so kind, but so cruel?" She imagined her father again, saw him sitting alone on a street curb, his hair matted, his gray eyes bloodshot and rheumy, his hand held out to a passing stranger —to her —pleading for a dime, just a dime...But she ignored him and walked on. He didn't deserve her charity, he didn't deserve to live.

Claire closed her eyes, hoping to erase her father's pathetic face, and wearily leaned back into the pillow. Its soft contours became jagged bricks, the rough surface scratching her back as she slid down the wall, down, down onto the cold cement below.

"Are you O.K., Lady?" The voice was clear and real, a stranger's voice. Instinctively, she shot out her hand to push him away. Instead of rough woven wool, she encountered soft fur as Max let out an unearthly shriek before leaping clumsily onto the floor.

"Oh, Max, I'm so sorry. I didn't know you were there." Claire jumped up and scooped the offended animal into her arms, leaning up against the kitchen table to keep from falling until the room stopped spinning.

"I'm so sorry," she repeated. "I didn't mean to hurt you, Maxie. I didn't mean to..." As she settled them both back onto the bed, rocking Max until his quick breaths became a steady purr and his rigid body relaxed into her lap, the same questions echoed over and over in her mind.

"How could he be so kind? How could he be so cruel? How could he be so kind? How could I be so cruel?" She thought of her father, of Mark, of Daniel. "I didn't mean to hurt anyone…how could I have been so cruel?" she asked herself over and over again as the light of day became the gray of dusk and finally the deep black of night.

Chapter XXI

"How could I have been so cruel?" Claire asked the question of herself, but since the words were spoken out loud, the woman on the park bench beside her answered, "What?"

Claire had not known she was actually giving voice to the thoughts that had tormented her that whole night...the night she hadn't slept. Just thinking about it on her walk home after the session with Mark had worn her out and she had sought respite in a city park.

"Oh, I'm sorry...I was just talking...to...myself," she explained to her seatmate who had already stuffed her sandwich back inside its paper sack and risen to make a hasty departure.

"You don't understand..." Claire called after her, but the woman merely pulled her light jacket up around her neck and quickened her already hurried steps.

"I've done it again," Claire muttered, careful to keep her volume to a whisper. "First I hurt Mark, now I'm really acting like a crazy person –just after firing my therapist. I think I'm losing my mind." The last

197

sentence was spoken to a pigeon bobbing his head at her feet in expectation of a handout.

"Shoo–go away. I don't believe in giving to beggars. Who knows what you'd buy…probably waste it all on drugs or booze and your wife and children wouldn't get a crumb!" Claire waved her hand in the bird's direction. Instead of flying away, he turned slowly and bobbed off as fast as his short legs would carry him, maintaining his dignity despite the rebuff.

She watched as the bird headed straight for a little boy doling out popcorn from a striped bag. Unlike Claire, the child seemed willing to share with anyone in need, asking no questions, and placing no conditions on his salty gift. After emptying the bag, the boy walked over to a woman sitting on a nearby bench, whose face broke into a warm smile as he drew near. His gait was slow and Claire noticed a white plastic brace that ran from the heel of one shoe to just below his knee. The sight of this slight imperfection drew Claire back to the morning after that painful, sleepless night.

Just before dawn she must have dozed off, for there seemed to be no transition between the blackness of the night and the bright glare of mid-morning. After working out the stiffness in her back and legs, Claire had headed to the kitchen to make some coffee, only to be confronted with the mess that she had made of the bacon the night before. She forced herself to clean the pan and stove before indulging in caffeine. Bacon grease had splattered everywhere –on top of the stove, the wall, the counter she had so meticulously scrubbed the day before. The effort made her feel weak and short of breath.

"I guess this is my penance, Max, for being such a mean person." Her cat had sauntered in and was circling her ankles, meowing piteously. She reflexively pulled a can of cat food from the cabinet above the stove and was in the process of opening it when she suddenly remembered having heard the word "penance" in the not-too-distant past.

"Penance, penance," she repeated as she spooned the moist food into Max' dish. While she was rinsing the spoon, she was able to recall the person who had spoken the word to her. It was the Duke when they had met in the hospital waiting room.

"Penance," the Duke had told her, was the reason why he spent his days performing acts of kindness. It was a penance for his past behavior, for the pain he had inflicted upon his family.

"That's it, Max. Why didn't I see it before?" Max paused from his repast long enough to look up, but was soon facedown in his dish, licking the remnants of his breakfast. He didn't even notice his owner rush into the bathroom, run some water, brush her hair before grabbing her purse and leaving, banging the hollow door behind her.

"A new person, Claire." Nita had dropped by a few days later a bit concerned at not hearing from her sister. "What is it, sweetie? What's gotten into you?"

She and Claire were sitting at the small kitchen table. The windows of the apartment were open to the warm early summer air. Curtains Nita had not seen before billowed out with each passing breeze. Max sat contentedly in his favorite spot, paralyzed by the sun.

"Nita," Claire leaned forward in her chair at the kitchen table, bouncing up from the seat like a four-year-old child with a secret. "You'll never guess what I've done. Go ahead –guess."

Nita smiled at her excitement, knew that she was enjoying the little game of suspense and decided to play along.

"You ran the mile in under six minutes."

"No."

"You cut your hair. That's it, you cut your hair. It looks great,"

Nita decided to get a little dig in along with the fun.

"Good grief, no. You are so cold." Claire clapped her hands and giggled, then pushed back the dark curls from her face.

"You've gotten a job in a fish factory and are moving to Alaska," Nita teased.

"Close, but no cigar."

"Claire? Are you really moving to Alaska? I'll miss you, little Sis. Besides, you hate the cold. You'll freeze." Nita hugged herself and shivered for dramatic effect.

"No, silly, not that part. I'm not moving anywhere." Claire waited a few beats before continuing, enjoying the sight of Nita squirming in her chair. "But, I do have a job."

"That's great, Claire, but you don't even like fish." Nita beamed, but a moment later the deep worry line appeared in her forehead. "Are you sure you're ready for a job, that you're strong enough?"

Claire quickly ran her finger over the wrinkle, smoothing it with a slight pressure. "I'm going back to teaching. Special Ed. At the school a few blocks away." She spoke quickly to prevent her sister from interrupting. "I miss the children, Sis. And they need so much help...so much love. It's a miracle, really. It finally came to me what I needed to do and I walked right into the office to see if the school had an opening in my field. The principal, herself, was manning the desk while the secretary was at lunch...seems they are understaffed, like most of the city's schools. We must have talked for an hour. I was very open about my recurrent problems –figured it would be best to let her know up-front what she would be getting herself into. Turns out their Special Education teacher is retiring and they were having trouble filling her position. The school system doesn't pay well and most people right out of college don't want to deal with the social problems faced by city students. But, I told her, the more problems, the better!"

Claire paused long enough to draw a deep breath and for Nita to respond.

"Claire, there are some tough kids in this neighborhood. It might be...dangerous."

"Oh, Nita. Don't you see? These are the kids that need love the most. They have so many obstacles to overcome and I want to help them. I want to help their parents. It's my penance, Nita."

"Penance?" Nita arched her eyebrows. "What are you talking about?"

Claire debated whether to drag Nita into the convoluted mental process that had brought her little sister to this place, but decided there were just some things even a sister didn't need to know...or could understand.

"Never mind. The good news is that, after looking at my resume and talking to the principal at my old school, Mrs. Watkins says I have the job. Orientation for teachers doesn't begin until August 15 –so I have plenty of time to rest up and prepare."

Claire paused, reached over and covered Nita's hand with her own. "The important thing is that somebody needs me. Nita, somebody needs me...I can do this, I know I can. Max and I won't even have to move."

Nita bit the inside of her lip to keep from expressing any doubts in her sister's ability to follow through and succeed with her new plans. For, despite all her misgivings about Claire's strength, her state of mind, her continued residence in this veritable slum, Nita understood the importance of feeling needed. It was what drove her to the NICU once her children had left home. She squeezed Claire's hand and gazed into those once lifeless eyes. "Welcome back, Sis," she said throwing her arms around Claire's skinny shoulders and hugging her until she had to beat on Nita's back to get some air.

Chapter XXII

Exhausted, yet, elated by the memory of that conversation with her sister, Claire spent the next few hours sitting contentedly on her bench, watching the pigeons and squirrels, the children feeding them, couples strolling arm and arm, old people dozing on the benches. When a young mother pushing an old-fashioned pram walked by, she sat up and strained to look inside at the sleeping baby.

"How old is she?" Claire asked the woman, who seemed pleased at the question and stopped to give Claire a better view.

"Four months. She's finally started giving her father and me a little peace at night, but I can tell you the first few weeks were pretty hard. Do you have children?"

The mother's innocent question would normally have sent Claire into an emotional tailspin. Instead she smiled and simply replied, "No. But I hope to some day. She's beautiful."

"Thanks."

Claire watched them stroll away secretly celebrating the fact that she had not fallen apart. Only a few weeks before such an interaction would have been unimaginable, so deep was the pain from the loss of her own child. "I'm healed," she spoke to herself. The words reminded her of Mark and her first inclination was to rush home and call him to report how well she had handled her encounter with the mother and baby... Then she remembered he was no longer her therapist and no longer her friend. She had seen to that.

Claire gazed in the direction of the departing stroller until a ray of sunlight glanced off the small pond a few yards away. Blinking to dispel the dots dancing before her eyes, Claire checked her wristwatch for the time. It was 7 p.m., way past Max' dinnertime. She stood up suddenly, the dots now joined by stars as the blood rushed to her tired feet. She steadied herself against the backrest, debating whether to try and walk the remaining blocks home or just hail a cab. The ache in the small of her back as well as the thought of Max sitting in the windowsill, his stomach empty, settled the matter and she headed for the nearby street corner.

Claire had never hailed a cab before. She had seen others do it, but they always seemed to wave with authority. Her feeble efforts attracted no attention from the passing yellow cars and she was just about to give up and start the long walk home when a familiar vehicle screeched to a stop inches away from her feet.

"M'lady? Is that really you?"

Claire had heard that voice somewhere before. She bent down and peered inside the dark cab towards the driver. Beneath a flat cap with a shiny bill was a familiar and welcome face.

"Joe?"

"At your service. Heh, how'd you get so far from home anyway?" Claire was too dumbstruck to answer. "Never mind. Climb aboard. Time's awastin'. The meter's runnin', so to speak."

Gratefully, Claire pulled open the heavy passenger door and slid inside. "You're a God-send, Joe."

"I bet you say that to all the boys," he retorted and they shared several minutes of laughter while Joe pulled away from the curb and maneuvered the cab through the evening traffic.

After a few minutes of comfortable silence, Claire concentrated her attention on the back of his head and the face reflected in the rearview mirror. Such a kind face. What luck that he had been driving by just when she needed a ride. Joe must have sensed her scrutiny and looked up into the mirror. Their eyes met briefly before a honking car brought his attention back to the road.

"Something big must have happened to you since we last met. You look great…Not that you didn't before. But…" Joe stopped speaking, afraid he had offended his passenger.

"It's O.K., Joe. I know exactly what you mean. A lot has happened, way too much to explain. The good news is, I'm alive." Claire looked again at his face, whose laugh lines had been briefly drawn down into a frown but resumed their normal upward tilt after she spoke.

"Well, that's sure good to know." Joe tapped the steering wheel while he waited for a red light to change. Claire took advantage of the moment to ask a question.

"Has the Duke been around lately? Have you seen him?" Joe could tell by her tone that this was more than a casual question.

"Haven't seen him for days. But, you know how he is…he's disappeared before, but he always shows up again…eventually. I wouldn't worry about the ol' Duke. He's pretty tough." Joe pressed his hand against the horn and shook his fist at a truck that had pulled suddenly in front of the cab.

"Heh, come to think about it, I haven't seen him since the day they hauled you to the hospital. He was pretty shook-up, I can tell you…Oh, are you O.K.? Do you want me to stop?"

Joe could see in the mirror that his last words had upset Claire. Her face became ghostly pale and he could hear her breaths come in short gasps. "Now you've done it, you idiot," he muttered to himself.

"No, no, Joe. I'm…I'm fine, really. Don't stop. I just need to get home."

Joe turned his attention back to driving, choosing shortcuts that would take them to their destination as quickly as possible. He was relieved when the color finally came back into Claire's face and her breathing began to slow down, but he decided to keep his mouth shut until she was safely home.

Claire closed her eyes and leaned her head against the window. When she felt the cab stop, she opened them again and was relieved to see the worn steps that led up to the door of her building. Joe jumped out of the cab and practically ran around to her side, offering his hand once he had opened the heavy door. She took it gratefully. Once on the sidewalk, he moved his hand beneath her elbow for support, but she pushed it gently away.

"How much do I owe you, Joe?" she asked while fishing inside her purse for her wallet.

"It's on me."

"No, Joe. I want to pay you. Even a kind man like yourself has to make a living." She held out several bills, but he had already turned and started back to the cab.

"Yeh, yeh, whatever…" Joe called over his shoulder.

Claire shook her head and was about to turn around herself when a question came to mind. "Wait, Joe." Claire stopped him before he reached the street. "How did you know about my being in the hospital?"

Joe looked back and cocked his head. "Ain't much happens on Danvers Street without old Joe knowing… the Duke told me. Well, see ya'."

"Joe?" Claire stopped him again. This time she could see the exasperated shrug of his shoulders but could not keep from adding, "If you see the Duke, I mean Daniel," Claire hesitated, "tell him…just tell him thanks –for everything."

"Righty-ho, m'lady. Got to go." Joe bounded around the front end of the car, pulled the door open and jumped inside. He tipped his hat at Claire as he spun away.

Claire watched the yellow cab until it turned a corner, then pulled her tired body up the flight of stairs, through the doorway and down the dim corridor to the apartment door. It had been a long day, she decided, while fumbling for her keys. And judging from the angry meows resonating from within, Max thought so, too.

Chapter XXIII

"Well, if you ain't a sight for sore eyes. Come here, give this old lady a hug."

It was lunchtime at the diner. When Claire entered a few minutes before, she checked the booths on either side of the door and, finding them all occupied, took a seat at the counter. The waitress, who now had Claire locked in a bony embrace, had been so busy taking orders and barking them through the pick-up window that she had not, at first, noticed her new customer.

Claire was as surprised at being recognized as she was by the woman's affectionate greeting and, though pleased by it, she tried her best to keep the grease and dried ketchup stains from transferring to her beige linen suit.

"Geez, ain't you all dolled up. Bet you got a date." The waitress treated Claire to another conspiratorial wink before grabbing the coffeepot and heading to the back booth where a group of old men sat, one of whom was waving an empty cup in her direction.

"Keep your shirt on," she called to the apparent ringleader. "Be back in a jif, Hon," she threw over her shoulder to Claire.

Claire swiveled the stool slowly from side to side. Music was playing in the background but it was barely audible above the clatter of dishes and animated conversations. Nothing seemed to have changed in the weeks since her last visit. The air was still filled with the same mixture of frying meat and onions, coffee and cigarette smoke. The customers, some of whom she recognized, were just as unpleasant and demanding. The waitress moved from counter to table and back to the pick-up window with the grace of a dancer, not bothered by any surly comments or complaints.

Claire could hear her shrill laughter and the acerbic remarks she flung back in the customer's faces. Her bravado seemed to please them and it was as if they were playing a game or rehearsing a carefully written script, one in which Claire played no part.

She turned her attention to the gray Formica countertop, noted the same pattern as the table at the booth where she and Mark had sat. With all the human comedy swirling around her, she felt somehow alone and out-of-place. Claire began to wonder if it had been a mistake to come here, after all.

It was the day before school started. The teachers had only been required to attend the morning meetings, leaving the afternoon free for last-minute preparations in the classrooms. After arranging supplies on the appropriate shelves and decorating the bulletin board, Claire had slipped out the back door. She knew she would have time to get to know the other teachers during the school year, but this might be her last chance to return to the diner to thank the waitress for her help. Besides, she was already sick of hearing about her colleagues' husbands or wives, daycare problems, and potty training. Everyone, except her, appeared to have a family to go home to at night and Claire hated the inevitable questions about her own personal life, no matter how innocent.

For weeks, the diner had been on her mind. So much had happened to her there, though she had only visited twice. Claire felt a deep gratitude to the waitress, both for her kindness and her role in saving Claire's life, both literally and symbolically. Once her students arrived, there would be no time to return to the place where she had faced near-death and at the same time had truly begun to live.

"What can I get you, Miss...er"? The waitress as usual seemed to materialize on the other side of the counter, startling Claire.

"Oh, my name is Claire. Claire McKinney." Claire held out her hand which the waitress took after wiping her own on the dirty apron.

"Just call me Fran," she said. "It ain't my real name but it's what I answer to in here, anyway. Now, what can I get you?"

"Coffee, please. Black." Fran waited a moment, expecting Claire to order food to go with her beverage, but Claire studied the countertop again wanting to choose just the right words to express her thanks.

With her free hand, Fran pulled out a white porcelain mug from beneath the counter, set it in front of Claire and began pouring from the stainless steel pot she still held in the other. When the cup was full, Claire looked up at the waitress who was shifting her weight from one foot to the other like a jogger waiting for traffic to clear.

"I just wanted to…I mean…I wanted to thank you for helping me." She spoke quickly, afraid Fran would be distracted by another customer.

"What are you talking about, Claire? That's right isn't it, Claire?"

When the younger woman nodded her head, Fran continued on in a hoarse voice. "I ain't done nothing for you…just brought you coffee, is all…like I do everybody comes in here." While she was talking, she swept the room with her eyes, looking for signs of discontent among the patrons.

"Oh, but you did help," Claire said quickly, grabbing Fran's free arm to keep her from leaving. "More than you know. I'm not the same person."

The older woman placed the coffeepot on the counter and patted Claire's hand. "Well, I can see that with my own eyes…new duds, new hairdo…" Claire took her hand from Fran's arm and smoothed back her hair. In a concession to Nita, she had agreed to a trim, but it still touched her shoulders when she wore it down, as she did now.

"And is that lipstick or have you been biting your lips?" Fran threw her head back and laughed, a deep

212

rattling sound that seemed to disturb something in her chest that wanted to come out.

"Excuse me, Claire," she wheezed before disappearing behind a door marked, "Employees Only." Claire was alarmed at the choking sounds that escaped through the bottom crack and wondered if, sign or no sign, she should follow her and perform the Heimlich maneuver. But, before she could rise, the door swung open and the waitress emerged, grabbed her order pad from her apron pocket and headed toward a booth next to the diner's entrance.

Relieved, Claire picked up her coffee mug, blowing gently across the top to cool it enough for a swallow. As the warm liquid flowed down her throat, she could not help but recall her last visit to this place. It had ended in the Heimlich, though that time she had been the one choking. Claire wondered what would have happened to her if the Duke had not been there, though she had no memory of the rescue. Without him, she might have died.

Claire closed her eyes and allowed memories of that day to surface. They were mostly a sequence of blurred images and sensations. She remembered a song, something about "boots." She remembered feeling hungry and stuffing food into her mouth -but, next a feeling of panic at not being able to breathe that had sent her falling, falling through darkness, a darkness dispelled only by two deep blue eyes.

She forced her thoughts away from those unpleasant feelings and focused on the Duke, on Daniel. Several times, she had returned to Danvers Street to look for him. She wanted to apologize for her words that night in the hospital, which she had not intended as a criticism. Claire had merely wanted to point out that, unlike her, Daniel still had a chance to be there for his son, to enjoy his time on earth, even though it would be brief.

But, it had been clear from his reaction and the fact that he had not tried to contact her since, that Daniel had been hurt by her words, no matter how well-meaning. He was probably in another city by now, living on another street, continuing his acts of kindness, helping people like herself with no thought of being repaid.

After those few attempts to find him, Claire had given up, deciding he was probably better off far from her, far from everyone who could hurt him. It had taken days for Claire to forgive herself for inflicting further pain, but she did not regret what she had said. For him, at least, it was still not too late to connect with his child, something he would regret missing for the rest of his life.

So effectively had Claire pushed the Duke out of her mind, that this series of memories surprised her with a new ache and an even deeper sense of loneliness. Her eyes filled with unwanted tears, which she wiped away roughly with her napkin, angry at herself for indulging in "a pity party," as her mother would say. This place may not have changed since her last visit, but her own life certainly had. She had a job, a place to live, and for the first time in months, a future to look forward to. If she had to face it alone, then, so be it.

Hadn't she been the one to walk away from Mark once he professed his love?

"What's wrong, Hon?" the waitress had returned to fill Claire's cup and noticed the wetness on Claire's cheeks, faintly striped with lines of mascara. Claire hastily swiped at her eyes, determined not to fall apart again in front of Fran.

"Oh, I'm all right. I was just…just about to play a tune on the jukebox. Any requests?" Claire grabbed her purse and searched inside for coins while she walked back towards the lit jukebox.

"How 'bout 'Moon River'? That Andy Williams is a dreamboat…When I was your age, I'd have given a year's worth of tips just to be on a raft with him…floating down stream…into the sunset–clothing optional, of course. Heh, you, hold your horses!"

Fran was forced from her reverie by a loud request for more coffee. She grabbed the pot and hurried away leaving Claire slightly embarrassed, but with a silly picture in her head of a naked couple lounging on a raft as a ragged Huckleberry Finn poled them down the Mississippi. The tears of a moment before had dried and were forgotten and she studied the jukebox menu for the right code before inserting two quarters in the metal slot. Claire could hear Fran's laughter from the other side of the room and wondered if the backs of her ears were as red as her face.

She watched, mesmerized, as the record swung out from the stack and dropped onto the turntable. The arm holding the needle descended in slow motion until the tip rested gently on the outer groove.

Leaning against the warm front of the machine, Claire closed her eyes again, waiting for the crackling noise from dust on the record to be replaced by the opening bars of the song's orchestral accompaniment. She sighed when the sweet, mellow voice of the singer started to croon. She let it carry her back in time to her family's kitchen. But her mind did not stay there for long, skipping ahead to the last time she had heard this tune: here, in the diner, with Mark.

Thinking of his face, she let her body sway to the rhythm of the music. She was unaware of any stares from the other patrons, most of whom were too immersed in their food or conversations to be bothered by the sight of a dark-haired, nicely-dressed woman, dancing by herself in broad daylight.

It was Mark beside her in her daydream, floating down the long, lazy river. Why, when it felt so pleasant to be there, had she fled as soon as he told her how much he cared for her? She had been in love with him, too, or, at least the idea of spending her life with someone so kind and understanding. How angry and hurt she had been when he had blown her off for his next appointment. She had been shattered by the thought of being just another client to him, another "kaching!" of his professional cash register.

But, somehow she could not handle it when she found out his true feelings for her, the woman he had pulled from the edge of insanity and resurrected, redeemed. Or had he just felt sorry for her, responsible for this helpless, hopeless person whom he could protect for the rest of their life? Claire had realized during their last session that she would never know. She also realized that the woman he loved was dead and that the Frankenstein he had created in her place would not be satisfied being taken care of, being dependent. If she and Mark were to have a life together, it would have to be a partnership of equals and she doubted his love for her would last for long when he realized she did not need him.

The new Claire thought of Mark's face, his kind, focused eyes which had looked so hurt by her rejection. He had looked as wounded as if she had kicked him where it hurts...

"That's it...boots," she spoke out loud as the singer crooned on. Well, she had finally gotten herself some boots and figured out how to use them. All that was left was learning how to live with the consequences of kicking someone with those pointy-toes.

Chapter XXIV

"Good-bye, Ms. McKinney." Claire shielded her eyes from the afternoon sun, until they were able to focus on the small boy stepping up with difficulty into the yellow "Special Needs" bus.

"Good-bye, Jimmy," she called back. "See you tomorrow." Despite the glare, there was no missing the pleased round face of her charge.

"You bet!" he exclaimed.

Claire watched as the child disappeared into the bus then reappeared in a seat beside the window. Jimmy smiled broadly at her again and waved his stubby fingers as the door closed and the driver pulled the vehicle away from the curb.

Claire didn't know which took more energy, getting her children off the bus and through the heavy school doors in the morning, or preparing for their afternoon send-off. Even with the help of her aide, it seemed to take hours to gather together papers and projects, stuff them into the appropriate back packs, and direct flailing limbs into coats and gloves. Sometimes she felt like the Pied Piper, coaxing the slow procession of wheelchairs and spindly legs down the hall to the exit door. The hours in between were draining, as well, as she attempted to help her students reach whatever mental and physical potential their particular lot in life would allow.

The first few days of the school year had been brutal. Several of her students had no control of their bladders or bowels, and it seemed, between changing diapers and wiping drooling mouths, that she was no more than a glorified daycare worker or surrogate mother. How could she possibly teach anything, much less meet their physical needs?

But gradually, as her body adjusted again to the rigorous demands of Special Education, and as her pupils became distinct individuals, she began to delight in the rare moments of connection with their trapped minds. Sometimes, it seemed her students possessed spirits old and wise beyond their years. And, as the semester progressed, these moments became more frequent and more than outweighed the frustrations of her chosen field.

Still, she could not help but let out a sigh of relief each afternoon as she sent her children, as they had become, home to their parents. Claire had developed a new appreciation for the latter group, trying to imagine what it must be like to have a child that in some ways would never out-grow their dependence on their families. How would she feel if she were in their shoes? Could she find the love and patience she witnessed on her home visits? What if her own Rebecca had lived, but been damaged from her difficult birth? Would that have been harder to bear than the ache of her death?

Claire realized she would never know the answer to her questions, but felt some satisfaction in helping other parents deal with the reality of their own children's lives, no matter how compromised and limited. And when little Jimmy wrapped his small hand around her two fingers for their long trek to the bus, he became her child, too, and any questions at all became irrelevant.

Occasionally, Claire allowed herself to think of Daniel and his own little boy. She had returned only one other time since the start of school to Danvers Street, hoping to find the Duke and apologize for her behavior their last time together. She'd even managed to flag down Joe's cab as it passed. But, he had not seen Daniel for several months, only heard a rumor that he had returned to teaching and had moved closer to his old home.

"Yeh, you could have knocked me over with a feather when I heard the Duke was a college prof... Beats me why someone like that would choose to live on the street...But, I guess it takes all kinds." Joe had driven off with his fare before Claire could wrest anymore information from him, tipping his hat at her as usual before leaving.

Claire had given up, then, trying to find Daniel, but was pleased that he had returned to his profession and hoped that her unintended criticism had been the catalyst. That information, as sparse as it was, relieved the guilt she had felt since that night in the hospital.

Still, she could not help wishing that they could be friends.

Claire had made few friends on the faculty. She found the demands of her weekdays left no energy for socializing at night. Weekends were filled with grocery shopping at Dulaney's and at least one dinner with Fred and Nita in their home. Mrs. Dulaney had stopped trying to fatten her up and it had been months since she offered advice about how to catch a man. Claire's restored health and good spirits preempted the need for any such meddling, no matter how friendly.

Nita was astonished every time Claire showed up for a meal, not just at how quickly she cleaned her plate, but how much she laughed while recounting some anecdote from her days at school. She could not keep from comparing this new Claire to the pathetic sister she had rocked in her arms barely a year before. It was a miracle as far as she was concerned, ranking up there with the fact that her own noisy, unruly children were developing into pleasant, responsible adults.

Claire looked forward to her lively encounters with her nephews and niece. It was good to have a family, she realized, even though it wasn't quite the one she and David had dreamed of on their long walks together in what seemed like a lifetime ago. She hoped he was happy and looking forward to becoming a father, the kind of father that spent time with his children, listened to them and nurtured their growth into distinct and precious individuals, the kind of father she wished she could have had.

In truth, Claire had thought little of her own father since the day she had imagined him on the sidewalk, rumpled and unshaven, asking for a handout. If she did, it was with pity instead of anger, regret instead of resentment. She never mentioned him during her long talks with her mother on the phone. Like Mary, Claire had moved on, and wanted to spend little time mulling over the past, of which Cal was a part. It sometimes made her sad if her mind wandered back to her early childhood when they had been pals. But, she was grateful that it never again pulled her into that dark closet into which she had been thrown and had been forced to visit in her nightmares. She was also grateful that instead of her father's angry, sickened face, she mostly remembered his proud smile when she pulled in a fish, his gentle hands helping to extract the hook without inflicting additional suffering. That was the father that was still there for her. That was the father she chose to remember.

Chapter XXV

Claire stood a moment after the bus disappeared, until she was sure Jimmy could no longer see her. Then, suddenly chilled, she pulled her sweater across her chest before entering the school and returning to her windowless classroom. She was never eager to face the task of restoring some semblance of order to the piles of toys, crayons, and crumpled papers that dotted the floor, but knew it had to be done. Mustering her last ounce of energy, she attacked the day's mess until each item was where it belonged, where the children would expect to find them the next day. Weary, yet satisfied, she grabbed her heavy book bag and walked to the office to exchange pleasantries with the tired secretary, and to sign out.

The waning afternoon had taken on an added chill during her short time inside, and Claire regretted having left her soft woolen scarf at home that morning. Max had been particularly needy, curling around her legs as she struggled to get out the door. She could picture him now, wrapped warmly in the scarf she had left lying on her bed, but ready to leap down and demand dinner the moment she opened the apartment door.

Claire decided to put off stopping by Dulaney's for cat food, too exhausted by the demands of the day. Max would just have to settle for the half of a can she had hastily shoved in the refrigerator that morning. It wouldn't be any worse than her own dinner of canned soup and crackers. He would just have to get over it, she chuckled to herself, as she searched inside her purse for the keys before leaving the school yard. Afraid she had left them on her desk, Claire was relieved when she heard the familiar jingle as her hand closed around the wooden apple at the end of the key chain, given to her by one of her pupils before the Christmas break.

Without looking up, she stepped onto the sidewalk, and started off in the direction of her street, three blocks away. Her pace was quickened by the growing cold that was seeping up under her coat, and so she was thrown off balance when her shoulder collided with someone hurrying the other way. The force knocked the keys out of her hand and they fell to the ground, close to the curb.

"Oh, so sorry…" she said, reflexively, bending over to grab the key chain before it bounced into the street.

"Here, let me help you with that." The man that she had bumped into had also bent over to retrieve the keys, scooping them up into his large fist.

Startled, Claire looked up, but the angle of the setting sun prevented a clear view of his face and she straightened up quickly, hugging her purse and book bag to her chest. The man, whose voice had seemed oddly familiar, held out his hand and motioned for Claire to take back her keys.

"Good afternoon, m'lady Claire. So sorry to have caused you such distress."

Claire grabbed the wooden apple and threw it into her open book bag and had just started to hurry away, when she stopped and stood completely still. She could not believe her ears. It was Daniel's voice. Puzzled, and a little frightened, she took a step backwards, and tried to bring the man's clean-shaven face into focus. It was a handsome face, but one she knew she had never seen before. But, how did he know her name?

Unsure what to do, Claire tried again to resume her journey home, but the man barred her path, gently grabbing her upper arm so that she could not move. He was so close to her that she could smell his spicy after shave and could feel his warm breath on the top of her head.

"Claire," he said gently.

Beginning to panic, Claire debated whether to cry for help. But, the man's voice evoked such deep and comforting memories that she forced herself to look once more at his face. Slowly, curiosity began to replace panic as she realized that none of the features were familiar...except the eyes.

It was only then that the stranger took a step backwards, himself, and made a formal bow with a flourish of his hand.

"Daniel?" Claire stared at his blue eyes, remembering a game she had played as a child with a drawing board. On the cardboard back, there had been the outline of a face with no hair, onto which you could add features with the aid of a wooden wand. Once the face was complete, you could erase the details by raising the clear plastic sheet covering the board. Claire struggled to remember the Duke's face, mentally ripping away the imaginary plastic sheet.

It took a moment to play this game, but Daniel was patient until the frightened look on Claire's face was replaced with that of recognition. She began to see what was impossible before -the face of a friend.

Daniel was the one caught off guard when Claire's book bag thumped loudly on the sidewalk and she flung her arms around his shoulders, pulling him into a hug so strong it nearly took his breath away. But, he quickly recovered, and wrapped his own arms around her thin shoulders. They stood there as if frozen together by the wintry air. It was not until a nearby car horn startled them back to the present moment, that they pulled apart abruptly, each suddenly aware of where they were -beside a public street at rush hour. Still, neither made an attempt to walk away.

Claire broke the silence first.

"I'm so glad to see you. I wondered where you'd gone...if you were all right." The last words were muffled by feelings she could not suppress.

"Away," he said. "As far away as possible from my wife, my son, from you...As far as possible from myself."

Claire turned her head, towards the street where cars and trucks were passing -where pedestrians on the sidewalk opposite were hurrying to their destinations, squinting in the sun that reflected off the shop windows. She thought it strange that the world was going on as though nothing had happened, as though this were just another end to a weary day.

"Daniel, I hope what I said didn't…" Claire risked looking at his face.

"Shush." He placed a finger on her lips. "What you said changed my life. I wanted to find you…I didn't want to risk coming to your apartment again…my backside is still a little sore from our last encounter there…and I thought it might be safer to meet in a public place."

"Daniel, I'm so sorry. I didn't mean to hurt…"

"Shush," Daniel touched her lips again. "It's all right, I was just teasing. Anyway Fran, the waitress at the diner, told me you were teaching at this school. So, I swallowed my pride, and took a chance…I hope you don't mind…I had to thank you."

Daniel could tell Claire was still puzzled and took her hand, determined to say what he had come there to say, no matter how awkward. Neither of them could feel the increasing chill as the sun became hidden.

"I was angry at first, I'll admit. I thought you were different…that you wouldn't judge me. I walked the streets all night, hating everyone and everything… cursing the God that had dared to give me life, to give my son life, then take it away. There wasn't much keeping me from stepping off the curb in front of a truck…it would have been so easy just to end it all. Everyone would have been better off."

Claire watched the muscles in his cheeks clinch as Daniel struggled to continue, focused on them instead of looking in his troubled eyes.

"But what you said to me just wouldn't go away. And I finally realized you were right. My son was still alive, but I was already kneeling at his grave, mourning a child that still lived and breathed, a child I no longer knew because it was easier not to…easier for me, that is." Daniel put a hand under Claire's chin and raised it so she was forced to look in his eyes.

"And, then I thought of you…I thought of what courage it took to face a parent's worst fear, and still choose to live. It was then I decided to call my son – right then –that very night." Daniel paused his narrative as a particularly noisy truck roared pass. Claire drew in a quick breath.

"It was 4 A.M., but I called anyway. His mother answered the phone. You can imagine her reaction to hearing my voice. She almost hung up." Daniel's eyes danced as he recounted their conversation. "But, I convinced her to wake Thomas. At first, he didn't know who I was, and when I told him, he still didn't believe me. As a test, he asked me the color of his eyes. At first, I panicked –I couldn't remember, but then it came back to me. 'Green!' I shouted."

"Dr. Redding," he said, "you have just correctly answered the million dollar question. Congratulations, but you have to collect your prize in person."

Daniel started laughing. "He was so funny, Claire. He sounded just like a TV announcer. My son –who I thought could not possibly find any joy in his life –was so funny and smart and willing to give his old Dad a second chance!"

Claire watched as Daniel's face took on a pale glow. She realized it was partly the reflection from the shop windows as they mirrored the last edges of daylight from the setting sun. But, she knew it was also from some deep inner source.

"It didn't happen all at once. It took days to convince myself I was even worthy of such a child...days to find the courage to clean myself up...days to call him again and set a date to meet."

"But, we did. His Mom drove him to a park near their house. I figured she wouldn't speak to me. She didn't, at first. After awhile, Thomas got tired of all the grown-up tension and went off to play with some friends."

Claire tried not to move, not wanting to stop the momentum of this confession, but her legs were beginning to stiffen. Daniel noticed the slight shudder that passed involuntarily across her shoulders and reached up with both hands, drawing her closer to his own body warmth.

"I can see you're freezing. Maybe we should save this for another time," he offered, but Claire did not make any attempt to answer or move, merely shook her head and looked deeply into his eyes. Daniel swallowed, took a breath, and continued his story.

"I sat with his mother watching our son laugh and talk, roughhouse with the other boys. Occasionally, he got knocked down, but he was always able to get up by himself. Once I caught him looking back at us..."

Daniel's eyes seemed to be looking at something far away.

Just then, Claire's now frozen legs gave way and Daniel caught her elbows, then guided her with his arm around her shoulders over to the curb where they sat side by side. She did not object when he removed his coat and draped it around both their backs like a cape. Gratefully, she drew his exposed hand into her own.

"Please, I want to hear the rest," she said quietly.

Daniel sighed and drew her closer.

"I won't say the conversation went smoothly," he continued. "It was clear my wife had moved on with her life and was completely content to forget she ever had a husband. But, at least she would still speak to me. We laughed a little, cried over our son and what lay ahead for him…finally agreeing that it would be better for him to face his illness with two parents rather than one."

Claire held her breath, wondering how this story would end.

"It was my wife who suggested that I move back home –for Thomas, not for her. But, I told her no…I couldn't trust myself. What if I did go back and left again when things got tough? I told her I wasn't as strong as she was…that I was too used to living on my own terms with no one dependent on me But I promised her that I would try to get my life back together –get a job so I could live closer and see Thomas as much as she would let me and as much as he wanted."

Claire released the pent-up air from her lungs. It escaped in a white puff. She had been listening to this story with a mixture of incredulity and expectation. Why was he telling her all these intimate details? What did he want from her? But, his decision to move back closer to his family must mean he had no intention or desire to include her or anyone else in this drama. Still, he had made the effort to seek her out, to find her, he must want something from her…but what?

She slumped down a little, hoping he would interpret her action as an attempt to get warmer, not a sign of the confusion and dismay she felt at her own reaction to this tale of rebirth and reconciliation. Claire knew she should rejoice at her friend's new chance for happiness, something for which she was partly responsible. But, the front of her body still felt warm from their embrace. The feeling of calm, of safety, of being home when she was in his arms, would not go away. She berated herself silently for the selfish thoughts that dimmed her happiness for him and made her feel somehow homeless. Was this what he felt all those years living on the street?

"Oh, Daniel," she finally said. "I'm so happy for you. A lot has changed for me, too. Do you have time? I'd like to tell you about my new job. But, not here…I'm freezing."

Claire leaned away and pulled the heavy coat from around her shoulders, dumping it into Daniel's lap as she stood. He had to grab the collar and stand up quickly, himself, to keep the hem from dragging in the slushy snow at the base of the curb.

Claire's mind raced to find somewhere safe and neutral where they could continue this extraordinary conversation, no matter how painful.

"There's a coffee shop not far from here. Care to join me?" She tried to keep her voice even and light, a tone befitting someone who, after all, was just a friend.

"I have a better idea. The diner on Danvers Street stays open for supper now. How about we catch a cab and a bite there?"

It only took Claire a moment to process this question, calculating just how long Max could survive without food.

"Sounds great," she replied enthusiastically, bending down to grab the handles of her book bag that was still lying in a heap in the middle of the sidewalk. She offered her free hand to the Duke who threaded it through his crooked arm, and they started off together, moving as gracefully and in tandem as an old king and his queen.

Chapter XXVI

"Well, look what the cat dragged in!" Fran spotted the couple as soon as they had entered the diner, escaping the frigid night air. "Close the door. Don't want to let in Old Man Winter. He ain't exactly welcome here!" she chided them good-naturedly while pointing towards the empty booth beside the jukebox, with a conspiratorial wink meant only for Claire. "Be with you in a jif," she threw towards their backs before grabbing the coffeepot and rushing off to fill the empty white mug of one of her vociferous regular customers.

Daniel and Claire slid into opposite seats. This time, their table had been cleared and shone as brightly as if it had been polished. Claire stared at its gray and white top, tried to recall the last time she had sat there and had become lost in its cloud-like pattern. Daniel could feel her drift away and reached over to cover her tightly clasped hands, resting on the smooth surface.

"Claire…I…please, tell me about your job. I want to know every detail." His words and the gentle pressure on her fingers pulled Claire back from the edge of that all too familiar well. She was suddenly grateful to this man for everything he had done for her, for his newfound happiness that she was determined not to spoil, and launched into an enthusiastic account of a typical day in her classroom.

Daniel was clearly delighted by even the smallest detail, adding some stories of his own from his son's experiences at school -how well he was doing despite his physical problems -and then of his job teaching at a community college and hopes of going full-time next term. Neither one of them noticed the time pass or the glow from the street lights which now shone through the smudged window.

Fran had stood by discreetly the whole time, watching this encounter, and had decided to leave the couple alone until just before closing.

"Heh, you two, cook's about to shut off the grill. Better order now, if you want anything." Claire thought the softness in her face looked maternal as though she were offering food to two children who had made her very proud.

Once again, Claire was certain that the waitress had mistaken her relationship with Daniel, though she, herself, was unsure of its nature. All she knew was she didn't want him to disappear from her life...not again.

Fran tapped her order pad with her pencil, nudging Claire back to the question at hand.

"You bet. I'm starving. How about you?" Claire looked over expectantly at Daniel who rubbed his stomach and paused for a moment, listening for a rumble.

"Yep. Empty."

"I'll get you some menus," Fran said as she walked back to the cash register. "You have to eat, you know," she yelled over the clatter of dishes in the kitchen.

"If you want to live," Claire shouted back, keeping her focus on Daniel's face. At first he seemed not to grasp the significance of her words. "You know," Claire encouraged nodding her head until his eyes grew round with comprehension.

"I get it!" Daniel raised himself from his seat, still clasping Claire's hands, holding them even tighter as he repeated, "…if you want to live." Without diverting his gaze or letting go, he sat back down and for a few moments was afraid to breathe, afraid to ruin the moment with something so mundane as a bodily need for oxygen. Claire held her breath, too, as if guarding something fragile and rare, something that might evaporate if allowed to escape into the diner's superheated air.

"What do you mean, 'if'?" The spell was broken by the shouts of several hoarse male voices from the other side of the room. "Everybody wants to live, don't they?" "What kind of half-assed question is that?" "Are you two completely nuts?"

"Yes!" Claire and Daniel yelled back in unison.

By then, Fran had returned with their menus and stood beside the table with a worried look on her face.

"Do you want me to call 911?" she asked Daniel who was so caught off guard that, at first, he thought she was serious.

"No…I mean, of course not…why would you think…" he sputtered.

235

"Gotcha!" Fran shot back, placing the menus on the table as she winked at Claire, turned and sauntered towards the counter, trailing the sound of deep-throated laughter in her wake.

Daniel and Claire followed her departing back with wide eyes and open mouths. Then, feeling foolish, they turned their blushing faces towards each other, trying their best to regain the magic of the previous moment.

But, it was no use. Fran's laughter was too contagious and they both began to giggle like two little kids, until tears blurred their vision. Their giggles turned to uncontrollable laughter and an occasional shout of joy, which were soon joined by guffaws from the grumpy old men who were still holding court in the back booth.

The laughter from inside the diner was so loud that several curious passersby, on their way home from work, paused to peer through the diner's steamy glass door. Even the weariest of the group managed a smile. Then, feeling the cold, they wished each other a cheery "good night," and hurried away down the sidewalk of Danvers Street.

About the Author

Carolyn Orser Key was born in Richmond, Virginia, in 1950. She attended The College of William and Mary and received a B.A. degree from Northwestern University.

A published essayist and poet, her works have appeared in <u>The Hanover Herald-Progress</u>, <u>Skirt!</u> magazine, several collegiate literary journals, and <u>The Piedmont Literary</u> <u>Review</u>.

Besides writing, Ms. Key enjoys following the exploits of her four daughters and grandson, taking long walks in the woods, and observing nature from the deck of her Doswell, Virginia, home which she shares with her husband and youngest child.

<u>If You Want to Live</u> is her first novel.

Printed in the United States
25735LVS00001B/81